It was the Marshall's season for murdering; his night of the full moon, when every hawk and cat hunted until sun-up; the bare-fist fight where the marshall wore brass knuckles and his opponent fought on his knees. Then Adams would ride back with another man's blood on him, file a notch on his Colt and ask, "Now then, who's next?"

FRANK BONHAM
TOUGH COUNTRY

Berkley Books by Frank Bonham

FRANK BONHAM

TOUGH COUNTRY

BERKLEY BOOKS, NEW YORK

TOUGH COUNTRY

A Berkley Book / published by arrangement with
the author

PRINTING HISTORY
Berkley edition / January 1979
Second printing / June 1981

ISBN: 0-425-04851-9

A BERKLEY BOOK® TM 757,375

PRINTED IN THE UNITED STATES OF AMERICA

TOUGH COUNTRY

Chapter 1

AFTER HE CAUGHT the Frontera stage at Marfa, Jim Canning could feel the tightness in him begin to slip away. All the way across Texas he had been restless, cocked like a pistol, studying the platform of each railway station and peering at the faces in the lurching day-coaches. He was a tall and slender man in denim trousers and jacket, his dark hair cut short and his skin burned dusty brown.

In every coach he entered, he took a seat near the back, in case a hand should drop on his shoulder and a voice should say, "Come on, Canning. That parole you're packing is just a sandwich wrapper, now. Back we go."

Back he would never go. He would fight his way into Mexico with a dead deputy handcuffed to him before he would go back to prison. He had had, to the day, the amount of prison he could endure. The last thing the warden had said to him was, "We've got a hell of a fine record here, Canning. I hope you ain't going to spoil it. Nearly ninety per cent of our people come back."

"This one won't," Canning told him.

But after he took the stage at Marfa, his own country began to fold about him, and a sort of thaw started in him. He settled back in his seat. The stage crossed a yellow plain, climbed some foothills, and looked down on an arrowhead of mountain valley. Near its apex, just distinguishable, was the town of Frontera. Beyond the town was a silhouette of dark hills which rose to a long, flat ridge.

1

It was in those hills that he had his land, the only thing the law had been unable to take from him. He wished he could afford a month to hunt and fish and train some horses, to forget how to be a prisoner and start remembering how to be a man. But he needed money and time, and he was bankrupt of both. He had to have money to buy cattle, pay wages, and lay in supplies. During his months in prison he had worked it out—how he would fatten the cattle, sell them, and put the profit into good herd cows. Then if possible he would pay for the services of registered bulls.

He wanted to start his herd right, just as he was determined to start right with the people he would have to deal with from the moment he stepped out of the stage. Yet how was he to have peace with men who were bound to call him their enemy? If they had different reasons for disliking him, they shared in common the expectation that he would eventually mix it with someone and Marshal Mike Luskey would send him back to Huntsville for parole violation.

Luskey, he decided, would never get the chance. This time he wasn't dealing with a thin-skinned young character who would fight over practically any slight, such as a sneering reference to his gambler father. The new Jim Canning had majored in self-control at the Texas School of Patience, Huntsville prison. Kindly instructors with hickory clubs had taught him how to keep his mouth shut and his face blank.

Remember that, he instructed himself: Have a smile even for the men who had sat on that prejudice-ridden jury, men who had decided that in defending himself against a man who had drawn a gun on him, James Canning was somehow guilty of felonious assault. They smiled at his story of self-defense because they had never really trusted, nor forgiven, his father. It had not gone down well with envious or religious folks that a gambler should hit town one night with a trunk, a deck of cards, and an eleven-year-old boy, and before morning own a prosperous ranch. And name that ranch Three Deuces, after the hand that had won it.

But most of all, he lectured himself, with the knocking of an old anger against his ribs, most of all be patient with Mott Wingard. After all, the land Jim's father won from him was the first range Wingard had ever owned. It had sentimental value as well as being excellent range, and its loss left him with a mere two hundred thousand acres of land. And on top of that there was the terrible thing Jim had done to his son, Ed—the crime for which he had gone to prison.

He had driven the claw of a fence tool through Ed's hand and permanently crippled it, the hand shrinking until it was pink and infantile, like a baby's. What a tragic thing that never again could Ed pull a Colt on a man as he had on Jim.

The dry heat of those trial days began to flare in his mind again. Slow down, he warned himself. You're not that far away from Huntsville. The thing to do was to try to believe the transcript of the trial: that he had been cutting a Wingard fence when Ed and his father's foreman caught him. That Ed had laid his hand on the butt of his revolver to strengthen his order to cease and desist. But Jim, it was claimed, pretended to believe he was being attacked, and threw the fence tool at young Wingard. The fact that the fence had been moved into Jim's land after the death of his father proved inadmissible, since it was claimed to have nothing to do with the actual attack.

Judge Henry Allan Coe, who had been friendly with Jim and his father, though not friendly enough to defend Jim as his attorney, gave him the minimum sentence.

That, Jim reminded himself, is all you better remember about it.

The blare of the stage conductor's horn roused him from his thoughts. In the dusk, Frontera was in view. It was a border town of gray adobes and ample shade trees, through which rose two church spires and a dozen windmills to look down on the parapet roofs. At the heart

of the town were some taller buildings. The stage crossed
a bridge and was on the main street. It rolled a few blocks
and slowed, and he could see the team pulling into a right
turn before the stage lined up after it. At the end of this
block was the depot.

With a blue bandanna, he wiped the dust from his face
and rubbed the film from his teeth. He felt as dirty and stiff
as he used to on the last day of roundup, and he wished that
what was ahead was as simple as a cow hunt. How to raise
money in a bank where Mott Wingard was an officer.
How to hire hands in a town where Wingard's disapproval
meant a freeze-out. Above all, how to retrieve his land
from Wingard, who had been leasing it while he was in
prison.

The lease in itself spoke of Wingard's power. He had bid
on Jim's land after the trial, and dared anyone to better the
offer he had made. No one did and Jim, pressured by the
need for money to pay his lawyer and knowing Wingard
would use the land anyway, gave over the lease.

The stage halted, hostlers came through a gate in an
adobe wall, and with wooden creakings the coach tipped
as the driver and conductor dismounted. The conductor
opened the door on the street side.

"This is it," he announced. "Good meals at the
Capitol Hotel, first block up. Everybody that's going on
be back in forty minutes. Take your claim checks inside
for your baggage, please."

There were five other passengers in the coach. Jim
waited while they dismounted. Presently a man in overalls
put his head in the door. "Mister, I've got to sweep this
thing out."

With reluctance, Jim stepped down.

Chapter 2

JUDGE HENRY ALLAN COE had looked up wearily from his desk when he heard the stage coming along Houston Street. It was six o'clock and he was hoping to leave by seven. He had a heavy law practice, mostly land and probate work, and there was little that he was able to delegate to anyone else. He had shelves of cigar boxes crammed with memoranda, each box bearing the name of a client. There was even one for Jim Canning, whose father's estate he had probated.

It was a curious thing, he thought, that he should have had it on his desk at the moment when he heard the stage horn. The judge had been notified some time ago that Canning was being paroled, and the call was a special one which the conductor had agreed to sound if Canning came back by stage.

At once Coe leaned back and removed his spectacles. For months his heart had been gathering that single hammer-stroke of shock. He was a stocky man with sandy hair and thick arms and hands, looking more like a middle-aged ranch foreman than a lawyer. Suddenly he stirred, disgusted with his own nervousness.

What's the matter with you? he thought. You never had the weak trembles before over a man getting out on parole.

But never before had he sent to prison a man he had known and liked so well as he had Jim Canning. He recalled what young Canning had said when asked if there was anything he had to say before sentence was passed.

Gazing indifferently at the judge and then at Ed Wingard, he had said carelessly in Spanish, "I'll be back . . ."

"As a wiser man, Jim, than you are now, I hope," retorted the judge.

"Oh, I'm learning something every day."

I'll be back . . . A threat, of course, but a threat for the whole town of Frontera, which had never made Jim or his late father welcome. And that was too bad, because they had simply accepted the weapons Mott Wingard had handed them in what was really his private feud. Wingard was liked and respected in this country, or at least no one was ready to step up and say that he *didn't* like and respect him. However you made your money, Coe had noticed, it was bound to look good on you.

He walked to a window of his office, which was upstairs above the Capitol Hotel. The stage was not in view, but he could see horses and buggies pulling over as the stage approached. Suddenly he noticed a man and a young woman before the apothecary shop across the street.

Damn Ed Wingard, he thought. Must he be hanging around town the very hour Jim Canning came home? Wingard stood there alert as a bird dog, tall and lithe and wearing yellow boots, a gray suit, and a black Stetson far back on his head. His right hand, permanently injured in the fight with Canning, was tucked into his pocket. Sympathy for him never entered the judge's head. The injury hadn't warped Ed's mind: it had intensified the things already wrong with it—egotism, intemperance, and an excess of sensitivity.

Running hot, the stage came on in a rolling haze of West Texas dust, its luggage piled on the deck under a tarpaulin. As it passed, the girl with Ed Wingard tried to draw him into the doorway, but Ed jerked his arm away. Coe recognized the girl—Ann Neeley, Dr. John Neeley's daughter.

The stage slowed with a gritty sound of brakes and the team minced into a tight turn down the dusty furrows of Clay Street. Ed Wingard turned and sauntered after it.

You damned fool, thought Coe. I should have sent you to Huntsville too. But Ed was the man with the injury and the witnesses; and even the judge had not been sure where justice lay.

He knew Jim had always taken pleasure in making an ass of young Wingard, which wasn't hard. And if he had prodded Ed into pulling a gun on him that day, then the rights and wrongs of the case were sufficiently confused to make Henry Coe decide he did not want to defend Jim.

Now what? thought the judge anxiously. Suddenly he took a forty-four revolver from a drawer in his desk. Just then the door opened downstairs. Coe laid the gun down and sank back in the chair. He could feel his scalp tighten as someone came up the stairs. In a moment the door opened. His heart gave a surge and then slowed. It was Ann Neeley who stood in the doorway.

Standing there, she gazed across the big, high-ceilinged room at the judge. She was a tall, slender girl with a fine figure. Her hair was brown with glints of russet.

"Judge, it's Jim Canning!" she said. "He's on the stage, and Ed's gone over to the depot to make trouble!"

"What's Ed got in mind?" asked Coe with a coolness he didn't feel.

"I don't know. But I know what Jim will *think* he has in mind when he sees him. And Jim may well be right."

With his coarse nose, wrinkled eyelids, and round spectacles riding his forehead, Henry Coe looked weary and perplexed.

"I don't know what *I* can do!" he argued.

The girl glanced at the gun. "But you were planning on doing something, weren't you?"

"All right, Ann!" sighed the judge. "We'll have a look."

"All this concern over Jim Canning is a little odd," he said as they started down the stairs, "for a girl who never had much to do with him before he went to prison. Is this for Ed's sake or Jim's?"

"I suppose it's for both of them."

"In other words, you're voting both tickets?" He felt bound to jostle her a bit. The Neeleys had been cool to him ever since he sent Canning to prison.

Ann flashed a glance at him. "I like Ed, and I want to see him get hold of himself. Losing the use of his hand was more of a shock to him than some people realize. As far as Jim is concerned, I've hardly talked alone to him a dozen times in my life. But I've written to him while he was in prison and in a way I think I really know him now. But I knew him well enough before to realize he had a case too. Probably Ed did pull a gun on him, though I suspect Jim pushed him into it. But if he pulled a gun at all, then Jim should never have gone to prison."

"However," Coe reminded her, "that's not the way the witnesses said it happened. Tom Elrod and that other Walking W fellow backed Ed up on his story."

"How else could they testify and keep their jobs?"

"If a witness is lying, it's up to somebody's lawyer to make the jury realize it."

"What if somebody's lawyer wouldn't take the case? And he had to hire an incompetent from out of town? Is it still called justice?"

Coe took her arm to help her across the street. Like everyone else in Frontera, she knew that Canning had asked him to disqualify himself as trial judge in order to defend him. "Why isn't it justice, if his own lawyer turned him down with good reason?"

She did not reply. They reached the far walk and turned the corner. He felt tension gathering in her as they walked toward the depot. "Oh, it's not so bad as all this," Coe said. "After all, Marshal Adams won't be far off. Since he put a ring in this town's nose he hasn't had much to do but meet the stage and look for faces he might remember from old dodgers. He's just about run out of badmen."

"Badmen! Shirtless smugglers and poor old cowboys drinking to ease their aches and pains."

"Don't sell him short. He's taken off plenty of blood and hair in tougher towns than this."

Nevertheless, Coe wished Marshal Luskey hadn't moved down to the river to farm. Luskey had hired this man Adams as his deputy, and when he quit Adams had moved up to take his place. Luskey was just a halfwit bellowing into a barrel, but when things were rocking along smoothly he never got restless and went out looking for trouble.

They gazed down Clay Street toward the stage station. Ahead of them the road sloped away under an arch of big Indian laurel trees with whitewashed trunks and exposed roots tilting the boardwalks. At the end of the block the stagecoach was being unloaded. Dust, shade, and the smoke of supper fires made everything as indistinct as an old memory. People were moving from the stage to the depot. Coe saw Ed Wingard standing by the waiting-room door. But he did not see Marshal Adams.

"Ann," he said, changing his mind, "why don't you wait here? Perhaps if I kind of talk—"

"No," she said faintly but firmly. "Since the marshal isn't there, *someone* had better be. But I think we should hurry."

Even the air of a man's home town felt different, Jim Canning was thinking as he stood on the walk. In the cool evening it was crisp and invigorating. The scent of charcoal fires came to him with a forgotten taste of dust. The sounds and odors and the bite of high-country air brought back an old mood. *This is the place*, he used to think, whatever may have been bothering him before, *this is worth having*. Perhaps that was what had kept his father going during those early days when he knew he would have nothing but trouble if he tried to stick it out.

Then he saw a man move from the wall of the depot where he had been leaning. He was slim and tall in a gray suit and a black Stetson with a silver lanyard. The hat rested on the back of his head so that his curly blond hair was visible. As he sauntered toward Jim he kept one hand in his pocket, while the other rested against his hipbone above a yellowed ivory gun butt. Then Jim recognized him, and retreated a step to the edge of the walk. "No gun, Ed," he said, exhibiting his hands.

"No gun?" Wingard repeated. "Get your mind off brawling, boy. Didn't they teach you anything over there?"

Yes, they taught me to keep my mouth shut, thought Jim; and he kept it shut while Wingard peered at him. The rancher's son had refined his venom until it was clear and hard as glass. He seemed to tremble with impatience as he waited for Jim to reply.

"So you came back," he said finally. "Like one of your old man's sleeve-aces."

Jim turned and walked back to the luggage-boot. He found the canvas roll with straps and buckles which carried nearly all he owned. He put it on his shoulder, but Wingard was right there when he turned. He had taken his right hand from his pocket and was holding it toward Jim. Jim felt a sick squeeze in his stomach. The hand was pink and shiny with small infantile fingers curled in toward the palm. It was holding a piece of paper.

"What is it?" Jim asked.

"It's a check. We're buying your outfit. This ought to put you in business some place where they like knife fighters."

"Ed, it's too bad about the hand," said Jim crisply. "Maybe the money would pay for an operation to fix it up."

"Oh, it's already fixed up. You fixed it. Can't hardly saddle a horse now. But I can use a Colt as good as anybody."

Jim had smelled his breath. "And I'll bet you're pretty good with those left-handed whisky glasses."

Then Wingard lost the glassy smile. His eyes looked haggard as he pushed the folded check at Jim. "Take it! Take it and pile back in that stage! You'll be at the border in a few hours. You can buy a ranch in Mexico—where they give medals to knife fighters."

"I've got a ranch," said Jim.

He was aware of men moving across the street from the Mexican cantina there, of two people on the walk some distance away. He was afraid to take his eyes from Ed. Within the coach, the overalled man was humming as he swept the floor with a corn-brush.

"You just think you've got a ranch," said Wingard with his teeth clenched. "You put a foot on that land, and—"

Jim gripped Ed's wrist. "Take it easy," he said.

Wingard's face convulsed. *"Take your damned hand—"* Jim saw his left hand grip the ivory butt of the Colt, and he dropped his valise and seized Ed's wrist with both hands. The gun must have been cocked. The tremendous blast of sound shook him. Smoke and dust rose about the two of them. Jim's ears rang, he could not even hear what Ed was saying as he hauled back, dragging at the Colt. Jim took Ed by the shoulders and turned him around, ramming him against the sandy adobe wall. Ed handled like a boy: prison had produced one thing, at least—muscular strength. He dropped his hand to Wingard's wrist and twisted the gun from him. Jim felt the throb of running boots in the boardwalk, and was suddenly panicky.

"Ed," he said, "that's enough for a starter. I'll be around awhile if you want to finish it up."

Ed's head slammed back and collided with Jim's cheekbone. Jim wrenched his arm high, and Ed grabbed a quick gasp of air.

"You're going to be in a hell of a shape if I have to break your arm," Jim panted. Someone clutched his arm and he glanced aside. It was Ann Neeley.

"Don't, Jim," she said. "Oh, please don't!"

"Talk to him," Jim said grimly. "I'm ready to quit."

A thick-set man in shirt sleeves thrust between them, and as Ed turned, caught him by the elbows. Jim recognized the unkempt, unlegal frame of Henry Coe.

"Ed, you drunken blowhard," Coe said. "Straighten

out before I have you locked up."

Wingard was staring at Jim across the judge's shoulder, almost weeping with rage. "Comes back here—a jailbird—like he owns this town!"

"Whereas your daddy owns it, eh?" Henry Coe said. "Now, Ed, this is for dead sure: I'll turn you over to Marshal Adams unless you turn around and get out of here."

Wingard's gaze settled on the judge's face. Then he looked again at Jim, filled his lungs, and his shoulders slackened. Tight-lipped, Jim turned to find his bag.

"Now get going," Coe ordered Wingard.

A moment later Jim heard Wingard's spurs clink as he moved toward Houston Street. He had an idea he'd be hearing them again before long.

The station master stepped onto the walk, a big bespectacled man wearing an eyeshade. Coe told him crisply, "I'll handle it, Vic."

Ann Neeley was standing there as Jim picked up the canvas bag. Her hand touched his arm. "Such a homecoming, Jim," she said wryly. "But after this, practically anything that happens will seem pleasant."

"And here I was with a speech all ready," said Jim. He looked at her. Her face was lovely, and there was a quality in her eyes that made it something very personal when she smiled at you. Perhaps her cheeks were a little too thin, her eyes too large, but they made her face even more striking.

Yet while he looked at her he began to feel foolish and disappointed. He had been tricked by her letters into believing they were really very well acquainted, but she was still the doctor's daughter and he was the gambler's son: they scarcely knew each other at all. And realizing that, he felt the bottom drop out of something.

Henry Coe came up. He did not offer his hand, and Jim was relieved, because one of the things he did not think he owed the judge was a handshake.

"Jim, you and I are overdue for a powwow," he said

tersely. "Come on up to my office."

"Pretty busy, judge."

Coe came naturally by a silent stare. It ended when he said, "Afraid folks might think you'd forgiven me? Listen, son, I turned down your case because I thought you'd pushed Ed into throwing down on you. I still think so."

He peered truculently into Jim's face. Some loafers from the cantina had gathered to listen. Jim cuffed dust from his bag. His eyes returned to the judge's but he said nothing.

Ann spoke quickly. "Jim must be tired, judge, but I'm sure he'll be up to see you in the morning."

Jim owed her a lot for writing regularly, but he owed himself something too.

"I doubt I'll have time for visiting," he said. "I'll be lining up some money tomorrow. The pay for making brooms and chopping cotton was 'way off last year. Then I've got to find some horses. I'll be crowded to make a crop this year."

Coe scowled at the men who were standing in the street listening, as though to flag them off. Then he lowered his voice. "I've got a little money looking for work, Jim. Not much, but it might help."

"I never borrow from friends," Jim told him gravely. "Many a fine friendship's been broken up just that way."

"Suit yourself," snapped Coe. "Going back to Three Deuces?"

"Makes sense."

"Tell you something else that makes sense—for you to get off the street. We've got a new marshal. I don't know what his trouble is, but I'd guess smallpox of the soul."

"We'll get along," Jim assured him.

He heard a horse coming along the street which intersected Clay at the stage depot. Coe tensed. "That's him. That damned parade-horse jog of his. Listen to me, Jim. Do yourself a favor and have a drink at the cantina. Then find yourself a room. But get off the street. I want to talk to Adams before he talks to you."

Jim took the valise under his arm and shrugged. "Well, I could use a drink. *Adiós*, judge. Ann, I'll be around to pay my respects to you and your father before I go out to the ranch."

"Do, Jim. And we'll go call on the judge together."

She smiled. She could melt ice with that smile, thought Jim. She could break rocks. But she couldn't make him like a man—any man—who had anything to do with sending him to jail.

Chapter 3

WHEN HE CROSSED the street to the Mexican saloon, the men who had come from it after the shot returned with him. It was small and dark and you stepped down a foot into the room. Jim used to come here when he felt like Mexican food or a glass of tequila. An old man named Vasquez ran it. There were the same dirty yellowish walls with cracked plaster falling off and bulls and roosters painted on them, a wooden partition in the rear, whitewashed like a hen-house, and some small red tables and slatted chairs.

Behind the bar on a high stool sat a short, slender young Mexican strumming a guitar carefully, as if practicing. He was rather handsome, with a longish nose, pale eyes and dark tousled hair. There was the shadow of a mustache on his upper lip. He watched Jim move to a dry place at the bar, lean wearily there on his elbows, and glance at him. The other men drifted to tables or took places at the bar where they could watch and listen. The young Mexican came to where Jim waited, moving casually on a stiff leg.

"Yes, sir," he said formally. "What will it be?"

"Surprise me, Felipillo," said Jim. "How you been?"

"Okay, señor," Felipillo replied, reaching below the bar for a bottle but keeping his gaze on Jim. "It's Felipe, you know."

"I know. Except to friends." Jim saw his eyes slide away. Felipe was one of those Mexicans who wouldn't speak Spanish to you if he knew three words of English.

He had decided he was better than Jim Canning now, and was letting him know about it.

Jim glanced through a dusty window. The marshal had not appeared. He squinted at the drink Felipe was pouring. It looked murky and smelled like sour library paste.

"I said surprise me, not shock me," he reproved. "You drink that one. I'll have something from the top shelf."

Felipe set the drink aside and poured a drink from a greenish bottle with no label. The liquor was as clear as water. He thrust it before Jim, "Yes, sir!" he said, and wiped his nose with a seesawing motion of the forefinger. "You're back now?" His face was a polite deception, but his pale eyes remained self-contained and calculating.

"I was a minute ago," said Jim. "How're your father and mother?"

"My father is not very well. So I am running things."

A horse stopped across the street. Felipe looked out. "Ah, there's Marshal Adams," he announced cheerfully.

Jim stepped back to glance through the door. He saw a tall man in a brown coat and trousers rein in behind the stagecoach and swing from the saddle of a liver-spotted appaloosa. He wore a black Stetson, and a gun was swung on his right thigh. He raised one hand and his voice came as a deep growl, "Hey, boy!" A hostler came spryly from the stage yard to hold his horse. Jim recognized the old symptoms of severe badge-fever—the delirium in which some lawmen fancied themselves on a first-name basis with the President.

He watched with a hard mouth as the marshal caught his thumbs under his belt and surveyed the street, gazing up toward Houston, then in the opposite direction, and finally looking into the Cantina Vasquez. Jim's fist closed on the glass. It seemed to him that Adams was staring straight into his eyes, despite the darkness of the saloon. He distinguished faintly a bony brown face under the hat brim. In a moment the marshal turned into the stage depot, moving with a sauntering self-confidence.

Felipe was smiling at him as he looked back. "Better, eh?"

"Why better? I've got no business with him."

"No reason, señor."

"Cut out the 'señor,' will you?" Jim took half the drink down. About three of these, he thought, and I can begin to enjoy being home. "Horse Hammond still around?"

"Sure. He's still down the street."

"Well, I'm going to need some horses."

In the back, at a table by a wash-stand, a man spoke in Spanish. "Horses? You want to buy some horses?"

Jim saw a man sitting alone at a table where a straw sombrero, a bottle, and a glass were the only furnishings. He looked about thirty and had a wide mustache and long sideburns. He rose carefully and carried his drink to the bar, a tall man with lean shoulders and long legs in tight leather pants. He moved with the dignity of a young tiger. He was probably too drunk, thought Jim, to make a deal even if he did have some horses.

"You want to buy some horses?" he asked Jim again.

"Maybe. What have you got?"

The Mexican's hand traced a design in the air. "Horses very fine! Mexican trained. *Muy listos* — just rattle a spur."

"He raises goats," said Felipe with a smirk.

The Mexican looked at him. His greenish-gray eyes stared fixedly.

"We ask ourselves how he makes a living," said Felipe.

"Ask *me* sometime," said the other man. He faced Jim again, the residue of irritation only half cleared from his face. He extended his hand. "Mario Ámador, señor. I have a camp in Conejo Canyon."

"So? Then you're on my land, Mario. It's only leased to Mott Wingard."

"Just a small camp. My few goats eat little. Who knows? Maybe people haven't even noticed us! You come out with me some time and I'll show you these horses."

One thing he could not be, Jim decided, was a goatherd. About him there was an air of having been spoiled as a child and now, grown strong, remaining sensitive and egotistical. But he was likable. Felipe's remarks implied that he made a living by smuggling. Yet he did not look like a smuggler either.

"First chance I get," said Jim. He finished the tequila and tapped the bar. Felipe refilled the glass.

"We have a friend in common," said Mario confidentially. "Judge Coe."

Jim glanced quickly at him. He wondered whether Mario was by any chance talking too much, for Felipe was listening intently.

"Judge Coe," Jim said slowly, "was a friend of my family."

"The same in my case!" said Mario enthusiastically. "At one time he practiced law in Chihuahua City. Chief attorney for the mines. *Ah, mire!*" he said, lowering his voice. "I want you to see these horses at once. You talk to Judge Coe now. Then maybe we ride to my camp tonight."

"He's just a goatherd," smiled Felipillo. "He's got no horses." He had poured himself a thimble-sized glass of mescal.

Mario pressed against the bar, tall and stiff, his arms hardening below the rolled sleeves. He stared with eyes growing narrow, glassy, and mean, stared hard for a long time without moving a muscle, until Felipillo's gaze drifted away. Then he flipped the glass of liquor into his face. *"Van las chivas,"* he said. "There go the goats." It was an expression which meant, *Here goes nothing*.

Felipillo froze. His eyes burned, but he was afraid to move. "Wipe your face, man," sneered Mario. "Your nose has been running."

Jim leaned down and picked up his valise. He set it on the bar while he finished his tequila. He hated to see a man humiliated, and did not look at Felipillo. He felt certain that Mario had been told by Judge Coe to wait for him, and that he had been waiting right here for several days. Coe would have been notified that he was getting out, presumably. He tapped Mario's arm.

"I'm going to be busy for a while, friend," he said. "But I'll look you up when I get a chance. Good luck."

Mario shrugged in disappointment.

For a while Jim walked slowly along the narrow streets south of the main part of town where smoke rose from low chimneys and backyard ovens and made a fragrance of dust and cooking. Like a thistle in his undershirt, a vague discontent was working into the pleasure of homecoming. His mind kept slipping back to the little fairy-tale he had told himself in prison, of how it might go with Ann Neeley. Hopeless men told themselves stories like that. Then they needed to dash cold water in their faces and wake up. What had wakened Jim was seeing how pretty, untouched, and perfect she was. What was she doing in a little town like this? Her thin cheeks and large eyes, her slenderness and grace seemed too perishable for this big sunburned country.

But damn it, she had written him.

Still, he admitted, all she had written was a sort of sisterly counsel against bitterness; an admonition not to let prison damage him, phrased in various ways. Well, he had come through the fire, but he was afraid the smell of smoke was on him. Pieces of the iron rod they had laid on him so cheerfully had broken off and lodged in his heart.

Hammond's stable on Clay Street.

Through the middle of the barn ran a sawdust lane with stalls at either side. Jim moved through the darkness toward a patch of lamplight falling from an open door. In the harness room an old man in a high-crowned hat was working on a saddle. It was wet with saddle soap and he was buffing the skirts with a rag. Under a lantern hung from a wall hook he looked hard and dark as a cinder. Horse Hammond was hard of hearing. He was not aware of Jim until he moved into the doorway. Startled at first, he gave a sourish grin and rose.

"How you doin', boy?" he asked.

"Passably," Jim told him. "Bad light to work by, Horse. Man your age ought to go to bed with the chickens."

"Chickens ain't got rent to pay. Came back to give us another chance, did you?"

"Yep. But you'll have to behave yourselves."

Horse said bashfully, "Good to have you back, Jim."

Jim raised the saddle, hefted it, and set it down. He took it by the horn and cantle and tried to twist it. The tree was sound. "Whose saddle?"

"Mine. I was just cleaning it up to sell. Damn sound stock saddle."

"I'll bet Noah wrangled zebras on this saddle."

"Age ain't hurtin' it any. Look it over."

As Jim inspected it, the stableman mentioned, "Judge Coe would be mighty pleased if you hunted him up."

"He ought to be."

"Oh, come on now, Jimmy," grunted Hammond. "You had a jury trial. All Henry Coe done was to pass sentence."

Jim held his sharpness an instant—because Horse had called him Jimmy. He had always been friendly, right from that first year when other people were calling him, *That cardsharp Canning's son*.

"He passed sentence, all right," Jim assured him.

"He could have given you twenty-three years instead of just three." Horse shrugged.

"Three! Just three! Do you know what three *weeks* of Huntsville is?"

Whoa, he told himself. Taking a breath, he turned the saddle over.

Hammond said gently:

"I know, Jimmy—at least I've heard—Sheepskin's a little weevily," he said, seeing Jim's finger testing it.

"No, I don't really know them things, but I can guess, seeing how they've changed you."

Prison had knocked the sharpness off some parts of his mind so that they would never take an edge again. But it had whetted other parts so sharp he was afraid to handle them. Someone might be hurt.

"How much for the saddle?" he asked Hammond.

"Thirty."

"All right. I'll need a horse, too."

Horse winked and led him into the warm, gloomy barn. In a stall behind a webbing barrier stood a buckskin gelding. Jim knew the horse.

"That's Luskey's, isn't it?"

Hammond pulled out his shirt tail and wiped his mouth. "He owed for board when he left town. He'd a took her right out from under my nose if I hadn't been watchin'. I've let a few boys ride her just to see what she could do. The marshal didn't know a hearse animal from a cuttin' horse. Try her tomorrow. She's yours for seventy-five. Oh, hell, make it a hundred for the lot."

"Horse, you've got religion," Jim said. "Me, I haven't even got money."

"Take your time."

"No, it'll be cash or nothing. If I can't pay in a day or two, I'll never be able to pay."

Walking back to the harness room, they passed a stall where an appaloosa moved restlessly. It was the horse Marshal Adams had ridden.

"Get all the police trade, don't you?"

"Try to. Mighty poor keeper, that horse. But no horse that feller rides will ever get fat. When he says whoa, that horse better set down and slide. Same for any man he decides to ride."

"Of course, if his name is Wingard—" Jim said.

Hammond chuckled. "Feller named Ed Wingard got dragged out of the Big Corner Saloon today and jugged for firing that shot."

Jim stared. "You're joking."

"No. His daddy's on the way in right now. He was branding calves out by the county road today."

Jim began to grin. "Maybe I'm going to like this marshal."

"If you do, you'll be the only one. Hawk's a mighty hard man to get acquainted with."

"That's what he calls himself—Hawk?"

Hammond pulled down the corner of one eye with his thumb. "He's got the eye, he says—for sharpshooting with any kind of weapon, and for spotting a man with something on his mind. He's dried up the smuggling so's you can't hardly find any sugar, except what comes down from Marfa—all the way from the East. And try to find any beeswax or decent candles."

They reached the lighted office. "Have no more to do with Adams than the law demands," counseled Hammond. "He can strike from any angle, like a horse."

"That's about how much socializing I had in mind," Jim told him. He told Horse good night and left the barn. Leaving, he felt the witch-hazel bite of the air and began buttoning his jacket. He had forgotten how quickly the heat died when night came in this thin air. Had forgotten a lot. The good mountain water. An ironwood fire in an arroyo on a cold night, horses clinking under hobble. The privacy of a million acres—not a padlock anywhere. It seemed as if, ever since he left, he had ranged on a long tether staked to the heart of this land.

When he reached the corner he heard the clip of hoofs. Jim stopped and glanced back. A moon no bigger than a hoof-paring illuminated the road. Straight up the middle of it, between cactus fences and adobe walls, came a horseman. At the livery barn he reined sharply through the big door, ducking his high sombrero under the crossbeam.

Jim stopped and leaned back against the wall. Horse was right: Mott Wingard had not been far. In a moment Jim heard him coming from the barn, the thud of his boots barbed with the ring of spurs.

Over his shoulder, Wingard called back to Hammond in his big authoritative voice, "Cool him out, Horse! I'll be leaving soon. If Ed's horse is here, saddle it." Head down, arms cutting a short arc, Wingard came up the dirt walk.

Chapter 4

WINGARD LOOKED LIKE a man with something on his mind. He did not notice Jim standing against the wall until he had come abreast of him. Then he merely raised his head briefly, grunted something, and kept moving.

All at once he stopped.

He turned and came close. He was a large man with a way of moving in to dominate you when he talked. An old corduroy coat hung from his shoulders, stained with grease and smelling of creosote. On the side of his head he wore a soiled straw sombrero. He wore one glove and carried the other. Gazing at Jim, he suddenly showed his teeth in a grimace.

"Couldn't get back quick enough, could you?"

Jim looked at him. You arrogant bull, he thought.

Wingard's eyes kept shuttling over his face. "What was this supposed to be—an ambush?"

Keep at it, Jim thought.

Wingard slapped his chaps with his glove. "They knocked some of the brag out of you, at least. What was this ruckus between you and Ed?"

"Get it from him," Jim said.

"Believe me I will. If you got off that stage hunting action, I can furnish it in hundred-pound bags."

Jim felt in control of his hatred. But Mott Wingard was strangling on his. Like all men, he hated to get mad alone. Finally Jim spoke.

"I came back to ranch. That's all."

"That's all, eh? Didn't Ed give you the check?"

"He's still got it, unless he's used it for bail."

Wingard's anger and leathery strength darkened his face. Angrily he seized Jim's arm. His voice rose. "Was jailing Ed something you and Adams worked up to embarrass me?"

The rancher wore his Colt on the left hip, butt foremost. Jim eased it from the holster before Wingard knew what he was doing. Wingard suddenly looked down and made a grab for the gun, but with an underhand flip Jim threw it into the road. It fell with a soft thud in the deep dust. In sudden alarm the rancher stepped back, his hands rising defensively as his eyes looked for Jim's weapon. Jim let his hands fall to his sides.

"That's for both of us," he said. "I don't want to get shot, and you don't want to hang. And I've looked down one Wingard gun barrel already tonight."

Wingard's hand came to rest on the empty holster while he peered into Jim's face.

"Ed didn't pull a gun on you," he said.

"Coe and I say he did."

Wingard's eyes kept digging at Jim's. "If Ed did," he stated, "I wouldn't fault him for it. Ever saddle a bronc with one hand, Canning? Rope and tie a steer? Try it! And watch the girls staring at your hand after it's shriveled until it's no bigger than a baby's. Then we'll see how you feel about the man who did it to you!"

Jim looked at him with flat cold eyes. "I did twenty months for Ed. Don't expect me to cry over him."

"Did you look at the check?" Wingard asked, after a moment.

"No."

"It was for five thousand. Do you want that, or do you want to watch me take the land for nothing?"

Something thrummed in Jim like a guitar string. There was a hollow excitement in him.

"I'll watch you try."

Wingard's jaw muscles hardened.

"I'll dicker with you. I'll go fifty-five hundred, and I'll even tell you why I want Deuces. It's for Ed. It will be all his, to bungle or make a success of. Responsibility— that's what he needs, and it's all he needs."

"There's other land," Jim said evenly.

"Sure, there's other land—but this land belonged to the man who crippled him. To me that would mean something."

"It means something to me, too. It means you've got two weeks to move off."

Wingard removed the stained straw sombrero and resettled it. His hair was thick and iron-black. He never took his eyes off Jim; he was studying him like a poker player. Jim saw him better than he had ever seen him. Back of all the stories they told of his meanness and free-spending, his brutality and strange kindnesses, was the need to cast the longest shadow in Texas. He would give you a horse you admired, if that was what would impress you; or he would quirt you out of his way if that would impress you more. In his heart he was as proud, arrogant, and lonely as a mountain.

Wingard turned without a word, walked to the middle of the road, and moved around until he found his Colt. He shook the dust out of it, muttered something. Jim kept his gaze on him.

Wingard holstered the gun and came back to the walk. And now he asked ironically, "Ever hear of a self-perpetuating contract, Canning? That's what you signed with me."

"I signed with you for a year. It's been month-to-month since. And you're four months behind in your rent."

"Oh, no," said Wingard. "You signed for a year— giving me option to renew on the same terms." Very gradually, his mouth eased. "Ask your lawyer about it. Ask Coe. 'On the same terms' means you're a landlord as long as I want the land!"

Touching the brim of his hat in a sort of go-to-hell salute, he strode up the walk with one hand in his pocket.

Jim leaned his shoulder against the wall. Is he bluffing? he wondered. Not when I can find out so easily, he decided. A cold anger swept him. If it was true, then Wingard had gotten to his lawyer and bribed him to write it that way. And if that was true, then probably Wingard had gotten to him even before the trial to make sure everything went right.

Damn, they could sure mess you up! he decided wearily. And there was no one you could go to for help. Everyone would say, ''Well, right-acting folks don't get into these situations.'' They did, though; and then if they didn't have a sharp lawyer, they paid for it. Coe was a sharp lawyer; but he was the one lawyer in Texas Jim would never go to.

He headed on up the block to look for a room.

Chapter 5

NOTHING HAD BEEN as good since he lost Three Deuces, Mott Wingard was thinking as he strode through the night toward the jail. For Cuero Ranch, as he had called it, had been his good-luck piece. Watered by Cuero Creek and some smaller streams, it was a big armful of land which had had the blessings of all the cattleman's gods—sun, water, and grass.

It lay like a hide across the southeast corner of the mountain valley and coasted on down the south slope of the mountains. It was where Wingard put a herd when he wanted it to come up fast. Under the winter sun, it was the last to feel frost, the first to green up in the spring. Burro grass and chino grass, Spanish oak and mountain laurel—match it! thought Wingard.

But in one night of whisky and poker, he had lost it to a tinhorn gambler. Ed had lost his right hand to Jim Canning; Wingard had lost his right arm to Canning's father.

Well, it was set up now. Canning would take the fifty-five hundred and be glad to get it. It wouldn't take much of a lawyer to convince him that the only stake he had in Three Deuces was the sixty dollars a section it brought in rent—three hundred and sixty a year.

And then he could at last give Ed a push in the right direction. His feeling for Ed tonight was a mixture of rage and sadness and affection. A man could handle anyone but his own kin, it seemed, for there his heart softened his hand. By this time Ed should have been ready to run the whole show any time it was necessary. But all he did was hang around town and court the Neeley girl. She was a fine girl, and he hoped the affair would end in marriage, but my God, he thought, Ed would have to quit fighting the whisky. In jail!

The jail was another block north, at the end of a solid row of small Mexican stores behind a broken plastered wall. By the time he reached the narrow door at the far corner he was moving with stiff, angry strides and his jaw was set. Inside, a desk drawer rattled as he touched the mosquito-netted door. Moths and black-armored June bugs clung to the screen as Wingard pulled it open. The jail was in what used to be a produce man's warehouse; the irritant odor of ground chili was still in the sagging beams. The floor was a step below the doorsill and the small marshal's office below Wingard was as simple and neat as a pistol. A rack of guns stood against one wall; there was a safe in a corner and a case of curios beside it—Indian pots, artifacts, some homemade knives and guns; and a roll-top desk at which the marshal sat, forming a cornhusk cigarette, but looking at Wingard with steady eyes. Marshal Luskey used to have the desk against the wall; Adams had moved it so that he could see the door without moving more than his eyes.

Adams said nothing. His silence irritated Wingard and made him uneasy. He was big—well over six feet—with a bony, olive-skinned face and a smooth, hard jaw. His eyes were quick and flat. He was a very neat dresser with an easy manner and a quiet grin when he was feeling good. He wore a brown pin-striped shirt and a vest with small lapels.

Wingard threw his hat at a chair as he crossed the floor. "Where is he?" he snapped.

Slowly and carefully the marshal rolled the cornhusk cigarette and put it in his lips. He frowned as he probed a slit-pocket of the vest for a match.

"He's sharing a room with a couple of boys," he said. "They had a pretty fair trio going a while ago."

"Damn it," Wingard broke out, "are you drawing pay to lock up every young buck that takes on a load and feels like making some noise?"

"Colt forty-five's the wrong thing to make noise with," said Adams. He held the match ready to strike, his eyes watching the rancher.

"Then why is Canning running around loose when Ed's locked up?"

Adams lighted the cigarette and dropped the match in a spittoon. He glanced at a revolver on the desk with a numbered tag tied to the trigger guard. "That's his gun, isn't it?"

Wingard recognized the yellowed ivory butt plates. He was unpleasantly reminded of the heavy fence tool, similarly numbered, which had been displayed during Jim Canning's trial. "What's that prove?"

"It proves Judge Coe brought it in as evidence. Canning took the gun off Ed, and Henry brought it in. I said 'What's it for,' and he said, 'Just put it in lost and found.' So I went lookin' for Ed—him being kind of lost, too—and he was at Pierce's joint, sloppin' liquor like a leaky rain barrel. He'd'a been in a fight for sure, only—Well, nobody'd fight with him, savvy?"

The rancher winced. "But Canning runs loose, eh?" he persisted.

"Canning's *way* up on my list," said Adams. "But with him it's a matter of what's proper. The book says he's got to call on a lawman in any town he stops at within twenty-four hours. If he don't make his manners to me, see, I'll drop in on him."

Mott Wingard grunted and pulled a clasp-purse from his pocket. "What's the damage, marshal?"

"We call it bail," drawled Adams. "The judge will set it in the morning."

Wingard's hand sagged.

"You expect him to spend the night here?"

Adams rocked his chair back and blew smoke at the lamp. "Do him good. Tell you something, mister.

You've got a regular damn whisky fighter there! He's had all the rope this office is going to pay out. If I were you, I'd haul him down to the hot springs and get him boiled out. One thing I won't stand for—"

"I'll tell you what I won't stand for!" Wingard moved so that he loomed over the marshal, tilted back in his chair. "I won't stand for any hundred-a-month marshal hiding behind a badge to pass judgment! By hell, if I want your opinion on anything I'll send you a form to fill out!" His mouth was frosty with rage.

Adams rose easily from the chair. His eyes were slightly above Wingard's. Wingard could hear his fingertips drumming lightly on the desk top.

"Well, now, looka here," said the marshal in a slow, reasonable way. "If it's just a matter of money, maybe the aldermen will give me a raise."

"As far as I'm concerned," Wingard snapped, "you're overpaid at any price."

"About what would be a right price?" Adams smiled.

"About the price of a stage ticket!" Wingard detected a faint sourish memory of liquor on Adams's breath, and he remembered the rattle of a desk drawer as he entered.

"I'm going to tell you something you've been needing to know, marshal," he stated. "You're about as popular in some quarters as a bear at a honey-gathering. There were one or two tough hands we could do without that old Luskey'd let bulldoze him along. You've got rid of them. Fine, but the whole damned town didn't need soaking in benzine. This two-bit smuggling and being drunk in a public place are illegal—but so are a lot of other things that we wink at."

In the lamplight Adams's brown skin looked tight and shiny over his high cheekbones. "Ain't had many complaints. I've rebuilt the county road bridge with jail labor and filled all the potholes on Houston Street. And of course I get blamed for no stuff coming up from Mexico, when their little ol' revolution would have stopped it anyhow. Maybe that's where you and me're different," he said. "I don't wink at any of them things."

"What about drinking on duty?" Wingard rapped. And tasted a sweet satisfaction at the surprise in the marshal's face.

Adams, raising the cigarette to his lips, said, "The drink was before dinner. The turnkey was here and I was off duty."

Wingard reached down and pulled out the deep bottom drawer of the desk. A bottle, uncorked, gleamed dustily among some office supplies. His mouth raised on one side as he grinned at Adams.

"You'd better cork that thing," he said. "It's going to evaporate before you finish your dinner. You see what I'm getting at, don't you, marshal? You could turn this old town inside out and never find an angel—even in this office. So let's not call the absence of wings a crime. Where was your last job?" he asked narrowly.

"Big Springs," said Adams. His eyes blinked slowly and dreamily like those of a lizard.

"Why'd you leave?"

"Politics." Adams blew smoke at the lamp. "Same stinking kind of politics you're pulling tonight. Laws are for everybody but you—or your friends. You have a hell of a time deciding how clean you want your town to be. I played ball with them in that town, and I've got a bullet hole in my arm because of it."

"How's that?" Wingard asked.

"Somebody's stinking relative. He'd done a stretch in the county jail. I had orders to leave him alone. One night he jumped the bookkeeper at the hotel, wearing a sack over his head. I'd been watching him. When I walked in he started shooting." Gingerly he rubbed his arm. "Doc says the hole may take years to cure up right. You can see how I feel about wearing kid gloves."

"Yes, I can see," Wingard declared. "And you can see how I feel about having my boy spend the night in the drunk-tank."

"Where's he going if I let him out? Back to the Big

Corner?''

"Out to Three Deuces. I'm turning the whole thing over to him. Canning will either sell to me or I'll continue to lease."

"Canning know that?" Adams leaned down as he asked the question and took a big key ring from a nail driven into the side of the desk.

"If he doesn't," Wingard said, relaxing secretly, "he'll damn soon find out."

The marshal jangled the keys. "Big responsibility for Ed to tell him, ain't it?"

Wingard smiled. "I've already told him. Though I judge Ed could handle it himself if it comes to it."

Hawk Adams moved to the grilled door which opened onto a hall lined with cells. He opened it. Wingard had a glimpse of a hall as solid and dark as a powder magazine. Adams turned back. Wingard was aware of the breadth of his shoulders and the lazy, cocksure way he carried himself.

"You know what I bet?" said the marshal. "I bet I can handle you and your boy all at once, if he gets into the cookie jar again. I'll slap him in a cell and hold him without bail. And the next time you swing your weight at me, Mister Wingard, I'll make a report of it."

"Why not make a report of it now?"

Adams's fingers drummed the air as they hung beside the seams of his trousers. "Never did like huntin' quail with a thirty-thirty," he said. Then he walked into the hall with the keys jangling at his side.

Wingard waited outside until Ed came from the marshal's office. Ed set his hat on the side of his head and the moon gleamed on the silver cord as he tightened the lanyard.

"Let's go," grunted Wingard.

Ed sauntered after him. Wingard had to slow his stride.

"Where we goin'?"

"To camp. I'm branding calves at Barrel Springs.

Dammit, son,'' the rancher said, ''it takes a hell of a time to build a reputation, but you can dynamite one overnight.'' He looked angrily at Ed.

''Then it's a good thing you've got none for me to dynamite,'' Ed said.

Wingard seized Ed by the elbow and shook him. He wanted to slap him, laugh at him, or weep for his own failure in making Ed big enough to fit his own shadow.

''Moses and Aaron,'' he said, with a groan. ''Are you trying to win the West Texas jughead race? Letting that Canning outfit make an ass of you!''

All at once Ed turned and smashed his fist into the side of a building. Mott Wingard stood there, sick, as Ed drove the crippled hand again and again into the wall.

''I'll kill him,'' Ed said. ''So help me, I'll kill him! He took my gun! In front of Ann—the whole damned street—''

Wingard hauled him around and held him against the wall. A fierce and wild torment deformed Ed's face.

''Ed! Cut this out now! Somebody'll hear—''

''Who the hell cares! They'll damn soon hear after I catch up with him!''

Wingard clamped his hand over Ed's mouth. ''Shut up! We're standing right across from Coe's office.'' He turned him and started him toward the stable. A chilly mountain breeze raked down Houston Street as they crossed. The lights were hard and bright.

''Hammond's got our horses ready,'' Wingard told his son. ''You're going out to Deuces for a few days and get in shape. If Canning's on your mind, don't worry. He'll be out there sooner or later, and if there's any trouble with him, I don't want it here in town. This fellow Adams— With any other lawman on the job, I wouldn't worry.''

Ed looked at him with a twisted smile. ''Somebody finally get the Injun sign on you?''

''No. If I were afraid of Adams, you'd be sleeping in a cell tonight.''

''But you don't ramrod him like you used to ramrod old

Luskey,'' Ed observed. ''You weren't worryin' about Luskey when you sent me out to kill Canning—''

Wingard caught Ed's wrist and hauled him back. ''When I *what?*''

Ed attempted to strike the big work-tempered hand away. ''You don't remember? You don't remember telling me, 'That tinhorn's fry is askin' for it, Ed—go get him!' You don't remember that?''

Wingard did remember something like it; but he quickly put the bandage back over a small, unhealed memory he never cared to examine. ''And you took that as a cue to pull a gun on him?''

''How I remember it,'' said Ed, looking at his hand, ''I just look at these fingers.''

Gazing stiffly ahead, Wingard moved on down the walk, gripping Ed's arm. But his voice had softened. ''Ed, did you really think—''

''Don't break down,'' Ed said sardonically. Then he added, as if suddenly disinterested in the whole thing, ''Oh, the hell with it.''

Wingard gripped his arm, determined to rouse him. ''I told Canning something tonight—something you don't know either. That contract with him is permanent. He can't break it except by selling. So he'll sell. But to you—not me.''

''I don't want the damned land.'' Ed shrugged.

Wingard slapped him with a stern glance. ''You will when you sober up.''

''All I want''—Ed narrowed his eyes—''is two things: Ann—maybe she'd like the ranch, I don't know. And Canning—he's what I want first. Canning under my sights.''

After a pause his father said, ''Well, if things work out, maybe you'll even get that.''

Chapter 6

JIM'S EYES OPENED in a cool room into which the brilliance of early morning slanted through a tall curtained window. From the street came sounds of an oxcart crippling past and the dusty trample of a horse's hoofs, but in the room it was completely quiet. In the deepest possible comfort, his body lay in the trough it had made in an oat-straw tick. He did not want to move. It was the first time in nearly two years that he had awakened alone, in a room that was unlocked.

The sun kindled on the flimsy curtains and began to brighten the whole room. Across from his iron cot were a washstand against a wall, a chest of drawers, and a dark-brown door to a hall. He remembered coming last night to Mrs. Lee's boardinghouse, where he had stayed a few days after his father's death. When he had come to the door, she said heartily, "Your room's waiting, Jim. Breakfast's at seven."

Just as if she had expected him. He felt better for that.

He went to breakfast when he heard a bell ring. He had donned a washed-out blue shirt and a pair of old denims. His hair was stiff and dark, largely recovered from his last prison haircut. Going into the dining room, he felt gangling and self-conscious, and stood an instant in the door looking at the people at the table. Mrs. Lee sat at the foot of the table and Grampaw Lee, her father-in-law, at the head. There were two other men.

Mrs. Lee boomed, "Anybody here don't know Jim

Canning?''

She was a huge, hearty woman with a bosom like a pillow. She took in washing and always smelled of boiled wash. Mrs. Lee gave the impression of being under a perpetual vow to labor, and though she had a voice like a drill-sergeant, she was actually bashful.

A thin, brown man at one side of the table looked up at Jim briefly and went back to his food. ''Hello, Canning,'' he said. There were two hollows under his cheekbones like bullet holes; his hands bore the lavender stains of age.

''Ira's wife's away and he can't eat in restaurants,'' Mrs. Lee laughed: Ira Moore managed the bank.

''Glad to see you, Ira,'' Jim said to the banker. He didn't know whether this was a happy coincidence or not.

Grampaw Lee had already said grace, but after Jim sat down Mrs. Lee rapped with a spoon and everyone bowed his head again. Jim heard Moore grumbling as he sat with his hands in his lap.

''What've you got on your list today, Grampaw?'' Mrs. Lee asked.

Grampaw was a truculent old man with a spade beard. He fumbled an envelope from his pocket and read off the list of articles he was supposed to buy when he went uptown.

''Add this!'' shouted the landlady. ''Five pounds of dried apples. Ten pounds of Arbuckle. We got a new boarder, don't forget.''

Jim glanced up. ''I may be going out to the ranch directly, Mrs. Lee. You'd better not count on me.''

''Good for you! Don't let 'em whip you, Jim,'' she said. ''I'll stock up a little jist the same.''

Last night he had read the lease with Wingard and found the wording just as the rancher had said. He felt a sick sort of rage that he had been tricked. Still he wasn't sure. Coe could tell him; but Coe had turned down his business once, and he would not have the chance again.

''Well, if you're going to ranch, you'll be needing money,'' observed Mrs. Lee.

Ira Moore grunted and hastily pushed his chair back. "How about it, Mr. Moore?" shouted Mrs. Lee. "Going to he'p this young rancher?"

Moore stood frowning down at Jim, his hands pressed against his back, over the kidneys. "I'd suggest he come in and talk to us," he said.

"Why? Owns his land free an' clear. That ought to be good enough for a home-town loan any place."

"Ownership—and possession—are two different things," said Moore.

Jim looked up. "That's all I'd need? Possession?"

"Well—*legal* possession, of course."

"Wingard's lease has run out. Would that do it?"

"Talk to me after Mott Wingard moves off," Moore suggested.

After breakfast Jim walked the three blocks to Clay and Houston. He had sixty-three dollars in his pocket. Standing in front of Shackelford's big general store, he glanced up at the windows of Judge Coe's law office, green-blinded on the east against the sun. Then he gazed thoughtfully at the gold lettering on the windows of the bank, next to the hotel. Ira Moore came from the high, narrow door and lit a cigar. As he blew out the smoke his gaze crossed the road and met Jim's. He pivoted immediately and re-entered the bank.

You pious bookkeeper's flunky! Jim thought angrily. If he hadn't got Moore's point at breakfast, he got it now: Don't ask for money until you've proved you're as big as Wingard.

It took a man like Moore to point your compass for you. If possession was the whole show, then he had better see to arranging it. He had the horse and saddle lined up; anything else he needed he could buy at Shackelford's. He turned to enter the store and collided with a man coming out the door with a sack of flour balanced on his shoulder. The man reeled away and caught his balance. He dropped the sack into a half-loaded wagon at the boardwalk. Then he turned to frown at Jim.

"Excuse it," Jim said. "I must have—" Then he recognized Tom Elrod, Mott Wingard's foreman.

Elrod looked at Jim's dark cropped hair and began to grin. He was a stocky man, wide and hard and made to last, with a very small mouth beneath a flat nose, a cleft chin, a thick neck, and small ears. He wore a striped jersey and bullhide chaps, with a black cartridge belt and a big brass buckle supporting a revolver. Jim remembered when the prosecutor had put him on the stand and asked, *"Is this the man?"* and Elrod had stared at Jim and said, *"That's him, all right."*

"Make yourself at home," Elrod invited. "Take all the space you need."

"I always did," Jim said. "But no more than I needed."

"Well, you'll be needing a little less now. How soon you leaving?"

"Leaving? I haven't even unpacked."

"So why bother?"

"Speaking of packing," Jim remarked, "you'd better get at it, if you're quartered at my place."

"I guess not. I'm real comfortable out there," said Elrod, wiping his hands.

"You'll be a lot more comfortable outside. I'm moving in today."

"Be seeing you, then," Elrod said as Jim walked into the store.

Shackelford's was rather grand, for West Texas. The storekeeper had an instinct for knowing on which side of his bread he would find the butter. So being a Wingard man he had done well. Since Jim left he had bolted some stools before the material counter and installed some screened cases. There was a new two-wheel coffee grinder. Already a number of customers were shopping and gossiping in the store, and as Jim walked back he heard Ann Neeley's voice through the chatter of woman-talk. Seated on one of the stools, she was buying some material. He looked at her slender back and neck and the rich chestnut hair. An earring swung when she turned to glance at a pattern.

"Something?" a man asked Jim in a raw voice.

Jim brought himself back. Shackelford, one hand on his hip, an arm resting on a screened case, was peering at him with small irritable eyes. He was a sour old man with a thin mouth and a neck like a dressed chicken.

"Hello, Shack," Jim smiled.

"Hello," the storekeeper replied. "What's on your mind?"

"Provisions," Jim said. He gazed up at the shelves behind him, aware of silence spreading like an oil-stain. "Let's see—"

Shackelford interrupted in his raw Southern voice.

"Is this cash?"

"If it has to be."

"It does," said the merchant.

"Set it out. Add it up," Jim told him curtly.

Shackelford had pulled that on him once when he was eighteen. So Jim had ordered everything in the store, gotten it piled by the door, and then told him, "I'll see if I can't do better at Howie's, Shack."

That was asking for it; and now he was getting it.

He walked to a rack of guns behind the counter. "Let's see that Winchester."

A woman whispered something. Tom Elrod, hoisting another sack from a pile of provisions by the door, paused to listen.

Shackelford laid a long, steady look of his bloodshot eyes on Jim before he lifted the gun with one hand and placed it on the counter. It was stone-silent in the store. Jim worked the lever. "Center fire, eh?" Shackelford did not reply. Jim stepped back to peer over the sights at the bright rectangle of the door. Then he faltered. A man was standing in the entrance looking at him. He did not stir. As Jim lowered the gun he saw the badge on his vest. Marshal Hawk Adams raised his belt a half inch. Then he smiled to himself and walked over to the material counter where

Ann Neeley sat.

"How-do, Miss Neeley?" he said pleasantly.

"Good morning," the girl replied. "Will you wrap that for me now, Mrs. Shackelford?"

" Makin' a dress, I'll bet," Adams joshed.

Jim listened with his back turned, frowning at the rifle. The law said he could not carry a sidearm; but being a rancher he could have a gun on his saddle. This was scarcely the time to make the purchase, he knew; but Shackelford's thin mouth was grinning with moronic delight and everyone in the store was dying to get out and tell it.

"... So he pulls a bead on the door, and there stands Hawk...."

On the other hand, no one would leave until he knew whether Jim Canning had been cowed by the marshal's mere presence. "They sure knocked it out of him over at Huntsville!"

"No," he heard Ann say, "I'm making my father some shirts, Marshal Adams. Winter's coming."

"Make me a shirt sometime, Miss Ann," bantered Adams.

"I'm really not very good on those fancy gambler's shirts," Ann told him apologetically. "Mrs. Shackelford, I'm going to pick that package up later. All right?"

Jim heard her walking across the floor toward him. He turned, and it seemed she was smiling just for him.

"Jim, I've caught you this time. Father told me not to come home without you, and I won't."

"Well, I don't know—" Jim began. His glance crossed to the marshal, big and neatly dressed in a brown pin-striped shirt and brown trousers, a dark vest with lapels, and a flat Stetson with a horsehair cord. The marshal was watching with cool intentness.

"But *I* know! You're going with me!" the girl insisted. She took his arm.

Jim turned his head to tell the storekeeper, "Just hold that stuff, will you?"

They had walked only a few feet when Adams's slow voice said, "Hey—friend! What's the hurry?"

Jim glanced back. He disengaged Ann's hand and faced Adams. "No hurry, marshal."

Adams walked to the counter and picked up the Winchester. He opened the breech, tested the chamber with his fingertip, closed it, and squinted over the sights. Jim saw the dark, skeptical eye scrutinizing him. The faint pock-marks on Adams's cheeks were like the dents of buckshot in hardwood. The gun hammer fell with a click.

"I thought you'd be payin' me a call by now," Adams complained.

"I've got twenty-four hours, haven't I?"

"You talk like I was the tax-collector," chuckled the marshal. Shackelford gave a bleat of mirth. Elrod chuckled. "I hear you turned down an offer to buy your ranch, Canning. Think that's a mistake."

"Why?"

"Do you figure you can pick up right where you left off?"

"I can try."

"Hellin' around? Makin' trouble? Knife fightin'?"

Jim glanced at Tom Elrod, standing near the door. "It wasn't a knife. It was a fence tool against a Colt."

Adams laid the gun carefully on the counter. "Don't back talk me, boy. I figure you'd be happier some place else. That's all I'm trying to tell yóu."

"Happier?" Jim said. "I wouldn't know how to act if I were any happier."

Adams shoved back the glass lid of a case and took out four cigars. He tucked these into his shirt pocket, and stepping within arm's length of Jim said dryly, "You never did know how to act. I've been looking over the transcript of your trial. You made a remark in Spanish after the judge asked you something. How come Spanish?"

"We talk about as much Spanish here as we do gringo."

"Even white men?"

"White men too."

Elrod, standing with his legs apart and his hands tucked into his chaps pockets, said, "Well, *some* white fellers, marshal. What he said meant, 'I'm a-coming' back.' ''

"And what'd that mean?" Adams asked Jim.

Small, glittering lights showed in Adams's eyes. The fingers of his hand drummed the counter. Jim could see his strength straining like the muscles of a horse.

"Marshal, I've served my time," he told Adams. "Isn't that usually the wind-up?"

"It ain't even the start," said Adams. "Not if you think you can smart talk this fancy shirt lawman. Not when you hit town swinging your fists and set out to buy a gun."

Jim felt something like coils of rope dropping over him.

"The law says I can carry one in my work."

"But Hawk says you can't. That's why I think you ought to shove along. Because I've got a theory there ought to be just one penalty for assault with intent: Life."

Jim felt strangled by the anger some guards with short clubs had taught him to hold in, but hadn't instructed him what to do with afterward.

"I'm not looking for trouble." Jim wiped his mouth to control the trembling of his lips.

"Oh, you ain't?" said Adams. "Glad to hear that. Maybe you can change my mind about jailbirds. I always reckoned jailbirds belonged in jail. Always reckoned there was something wrong upstairs with a knife fighter, too."

"Will you quit saying it was a knife? I thought you read the transcript." Jim's voice sounded high and hollow, like a shout in an empty house. The nice, funny words they had for people who had troubles: jailbird—gimpy—lunger.

The marshal winked at Elrod. "Well, looky here! He's going to shout me down, now." That nervous right hand was almost touching the handle of his Colt. "He's been to Huntsville, so he's a real badman. He's going to stand right up and tell Hawk how it's going to be!"

A pulse had begun to squeeze in Jim's head, and he could not slow it.

"Man with the only gun in sight sure can make a lot of noise, can't he?" he said.

Adams reached down and flipped his gun from the holster. It spun in the air, blue and silver, dropped butt-first into his left hand, and with another flip he reversed it so that he was holding the gun by the barrel. His eyes commanded Jim's all during the shift of the gun. He jammed it into Jim's belly.

"Here," he offered. "Try mine."

The gun butt dug deep into Jim's stomach. He put his hand on it to push it away. The marshal swung his fist. Jim felt a ringing numbness burst like a cartridge in his head. He found himself on the floor, trying to push himself up. He saw a pair of boots with carved spur-leathers in front of him. Above him he heard someone say, "People reaching for things and not gettin' 'em is what keeps 'em poor. Ain't that so, Elrod?"

Jim's jaw was aching. He looked around dully. What he saw first was old Shackelford's face behind the cigar case. He appeared shocked. There was actually pity in the bloodshot eyes as he stared down at Jim. Jim's gaze trailed around as he began to put things together; the faces of the customers gazing down at him were stiff and frozen, like faces in a tintype.

Ann knelt beside Jim as he tried to get up. His limbs seemed separately controlled; he could not collect them.

Ann turned to the marshal and said, "That was the most vicious thing I ever saw."

"You just don't understand me at all, Miss Neeley," said Adams sadly. "I'm trying to run a clean town, is all."

The boots strolled past Jim to the door. He rose but had to back up to the counter to brace himself. He saw Adams pause on the boardwalk, raise his gun belt, square his shoulders, and drift across the road to the bank.

Tom Elrod went on loading things out to the wagon.

Shackelford produced a glass of rum and placed it on the counter before Jim. "You still want them provisions?" he asked quietly.

Jim drank the small glass and blew out his cheeks. The thickness was wearing off. "I'll just take what I can carry in saddlebags."

Ann put her hand over his. "Jim, please come down and let Dad look at your jaw. It's swelling. It may be broken."

Jim worked it. "That's just a Huntsville toothache," he assured her. How could you make a girl understand that she could not possibly help in a man's fight? "I'll make you a promise. First time I'm in, I'll look you folks up first thing."

Ann looked at him. She turned quickly and went to pay for her purchases. By the time Jim was through buying, she had left. "You know, I think I'll take that rifle," Jim told Shackelford.

The storekeeper watched him pick it up.

"Jim—I wouldn't dare!"

"How come? Do I need a note from my mother?" Jim asked. Then he grew aware of Tom Elrod behind him, drawing on gloves.

"No, but that fellow—he's all rawhide and sand, Jim!" Shackelford said anxiously.

Jim smiled. You had to get hit in the jaw in this town before they'd call you by your first name.

He heard Elrod telling the storekeeper, "Better make it a fence tool, Shack. He's pretty sharp with one of them, even up to a hundred yards."

As he turned Jim cocked his arm, sighting at Elrod's chin. He hit him clean and hard, right on the cleft of it. Elrod dropped, rolled over on his face, and pulled his knees up under him but could not rise. Looking at him, Jim felt exalted, like standing in a bright pool of sunshine and feeling on his face the first rain of the summer. Rubbing his fist, he faced Shackelford again.

"Guess that's it," he said seriously. "What do I owe

you? Figure the gun in.''

Shackelford did not meet his eyes as he began to add it up on a paper sack. ''Reckon it's more of a question what you owe Wingard,'' he muttered. ''Maybe you ain't changed as much as I figured.''

Chapter 7

"YOU'RE THE ONLY daughter I've got left, you know," Doctor Neeley complained to Ann.

In the late morning they were driving in the doctor's black wagonette toward their acreage east of town. It was a comfortable rig with a full roof, and roll-down curtains in back. Ann gazed at the hills which crumpled from the valley floor a mile or two ahead.

"It's people being afraid of losing 'the only thing they've got' that lets people like Marshal Adams move in on them," she told her father. "They've got a lot more than they think, but they don't know it until they lose it."

"Which might also be said of young women who jest at scars," returned the doctor. "But if you continue to act as nurse and counsel to a man just out of prison—"

"A man who should never have gone to prison!" retorted Ann.

Abruptly they were silent, adversaries who respected each other's skill at debate. A New Englander, the doctor could not comprehend that his daughter, born and reared in Texas, had not received an ordinary sense of caution as a birthright. He was a very small man who affected a goatee, frock coats, and long gray hair curling up off his velvet collars.

The shaft-horse trotted on along the road which trailed between the mesquite hills of Mott Wingard's range. They reached a line of craggy posts with five strands of rusty wire crossing the road. The fence marked the extent of

Wingard's loss to Canning's father on a poker hand. Beyond it they had Three Deuces on the right, the doctor's handful of lease land on the left.

"Would it be likely," Ann asked finally, "that a blow like that could break a man's jaw?"

"Very likely. But he'd know it. Stop fretting."

"There's something in Jim so—so fine!—and I want to see it come out."

"Let's see: how many ruckuses did your rough diamond get into that last year?" conjectured Neeley. "There was the steer he rode into the saloon just a week after his father died—"

"Because Pierce was whispering that his father had used a marked deck to beat Mott Wingard!"

"Who knows?" shrugged the doctor. "And I remember he cut off half of some commission man's mustache—and dared him to cut off the rest before he left town!" He chuckled at that particular memory.

"And you don't remember who the man was? It was Shelby—the same trader who sold you these feed-lot cast-offs we've been trying to get rid of ever since! And all he'd done to Jim was to refuse to pay for some cattle until the estate had been settled!"

"Jim's quite a man to write his own laws, isn't he?" the doctor commented.

Ann did not answer.

Off to the right a little blur of mesquite smoke rose from beyond a red ridge. They both looked at it, and Ann felt the horse pulling more strongly as the doctor let it move out. Mott Wingard had a small camp over there which was used as a way-point between Three Deuces and his own range. They knew Wingard and Ed had ridden out last night, and Ann was afraid of the kind of mood Ed would be in. By now Tom Elrod might be with them; and, thinking of the council that must be taking place, she was frightened.

Then as they were nearing their own turn-off, she heard a man shout. Her father glanced back through the dust and said sourly, "Ed Wingard. I wonder what's on his damnfool—excuse me. I wonder what's on his mind?"

Wingard hauled the horse in beside the wagonette. The pony brought its hind legs under it in a sliding stop, then Ed let it come out in a jog. He grinned down at them and raised his hat to Ann. "Miss Neeley—Doctor!" he said in burlesqued courtliness. Slender and gray-clad, there was a look of glitter about him, an unhealthy excitement.

"Mr. Wingard," responded the doctor dryly.

"'Bout time you were getting out here," Ed announced. "Those critters of yours are needing a doctor for sure."

"What's the matter with them?" Neeley growled.

"Some people around here think they're starvin'," Ed winked at Ann.

Ann did not smile. It hadn't seemed particularly humorous that the doctor's bargain cattle had come from a feed-lot, and, refusing to fend for themselves, were slowly going downhill. It was a good cow-country joke, except to the man who had bought them.

"I'll tell you who else is starving," Neeley said. "The fool who bought them."

Ed laughed. "Sell and take your loss, Doc. Things'll get worse before they get better. Don't you ever buy cattle again without letting me see them."

"Be sure I won't. I'm going to get the opinion of every man, woman, and child in the county next time."

Ed pointed at a slope northeast of the road. "You ought to cut those cedars, too, Doc. You might grow some grass there if it wasn't starved out."

With a hiss of breath through his mustache, Doctor Neeley shifted to stare at Wingard. Ann spoke quickly. "We'd be glad to cut them, Ed, if we could afford it. Anyway we're going to let the lease go next month."

Ed winked at the doctor. "Good. One rancher in the family's enough."

Ann saw her father's hands tighten on the reins. She flinched and felt herself reddening, but would not look at him.

"How's the hand?" asked Neeley, with the lack of curiosity of a man inquiring about the weather.

Wingard glanced at it. *"Poco, poco,"* he shrugged. "I was wondering. If a man got a cut like that, what had he ought to do to keep it from mortifying like mine?"

"In the first place," said Neeley, "he ought to keep out of situations where he'd get such wounds. But if he got one, he ought to keep it as clean as possible. If you'd come to me sooner, I could have done more."

There was a porcelain-hard intentness about Ed's eyes. "So it was the infection more than the cut, eh?"

"Yes. A palmar space infection is mean."

"Mmm," said Wingard, thoughtfully opening and closing the tiny pink hand. He remained preoccupied until they reached the turn-off to the doctor's camp.

"Which way?" Neeley asked him.

"I'm going out to Deuces. Canning may try to move in on us. Dad will be along when he makes sure the boys at the line camp have enough to keep them busy."

The doctor looked at Ann. "It's his land, isn't it?" the girl asked.

"But it's our lease," Ed grinned. "And riding that lease is kind of like wiping your nose on a hoop—there's no end to it. No way under the sun he can break it except by selling to us."

Ann was startled. "Ed, I think that's—"

"You think that's terrible?" Ed snorted. "What do you think about Canning swingin' on Elrod this morning?"

"I wasn't there, Ed, so how can I judge? How did you hear about it so soon?"

"Elrod just went by. He left the wagon in town."

He moved the fingers of his crippled hand, gazing across the hills toward Canning's home place. "You know, he's going to keep on crowding people until he winds up with a hand like mine."

The doctor's foot was tapping the floorboards. "Jim's served his time, Ed."

"But I'm still servin' mine."

"So is Jim. For the rest of his life he'll be traveling second class. No gun—report to the authorities in every Texas town he hits—Ed, he can't even vote! It wouldn't matter if he were St. Peter himself—he'd be a jailbird first and an apostle second."

"Amen," Wingard pronounced cheerfully. He drew the slide of his silver hat-cord up under his chin. Then he looked down with a smile, raising his hand in that same counterfeit courtliness. "Miss Ann—Doctor—the top of what's left of the morning to you!"

"He's very happy about something, isn't he?" Ann said as they watched him ride away.

"Sometimes," breathed the doctor, "I wonder whether Coe sent the wrong man to prison."

Chapter 8

Jim HAD RIDDEN hard from Frontera, but at Doctor Neeley's cow camp at the head of Cuero Creek he stopped to rest the horse. Mike Luskey's buckskin was a fine little pony but out of condition. He was rubbing its wet forelegs with a gunny sack when he heard a wagon clattering through a shallow trough between two flinty hills. Jim dropped the sack and pulled Horse Hammond's old Henry rifle from the saddle. Shackelford had asked one hundred dollars for the Winchester, so Jim had had to borrow a rifle. He had taken the horse on approval.

He walked to the old stone cattle pens, where he could follow the red scar of the wagon road down through the mesquite. In addition to the corrals, Neeley's line camp consisted of a *jacal* plastered with mud, some very old mistletoe-choked cottonwoods on the bank of a wash, and a few trusses of hay. Rusty branding irons hung from low branches of the trees.

Tall and sober, he stood with one shoulder against the trunk of a cottonwood. Under the brim of a new straw sombrero, his face was brown as tanbark. His narrow, green-gray eyes watched the wagon moving through the brush.

Suddenly he knew the wagon. He strode back to the horse and jammed the rifle into the boot. It was nice of people to be so generous with their advice. No doubt Doctor Neeley had driven out to deliver a short talk on the virtues of turning the other cheek. Perhaps somebody would lend him his chin next time Marshal Adams needed one to hit. For there was a clear tie-up between being long-suffering and getting knocked around. Battered were the meek, Jim had long since concluded.

Mounting, he looked back once more. He saw something bright as autumn in the little wagon. So unless the Yankee doctor was wearing a buttercup-yellow duster, he must have brought Ann with him. It figured, he thought, squinting. It figured, but still he wanted to see her more than he wanted to avoid another helping of advice.

When they drove in, Jim was waiting. Neeley insisted on helping his daughter from the wagon. She winked at Jim across his shoulder, her eyes very dark and her lips laughing. Neeley staggered a little as he set her down. He had the brittle strength of an old Christmas tree.

"Jim," Ann said, "you've had us worried. Disappearing like this as though you'd left the country."

Neeley wore a wry expression, as though Jim's leaving were something he could have endured. However, he pulled a stethoscope from his coat pocket and smiled as he came forward. "We're glad you're back. Why don't you stay awhile this time? Pull up your shirt."

"What?" Jim frowned.

"Let's see if you brought anything back from Huntsville besides some squint lines in your face."

"No use arguing," Ann assured Jim.

Jim raised his shirt and Neeley thrust the cold instrument against his ribs. "Get much exercise?" asked the old man.

"Well, they called it hard labor."

"Seems to have agreed with you. Apparently prison could have been worse."

"Nothing could have been worse," Jim said slowly.

Neeley looked up, the faded blue eyes faintly hostile. Funny, thought Jim. I thought he was on my side. Pocketing the stethoscope, Neeley said, "Then I'd see to it that I never went back."

"I mean to."

"Swinging on Tom Elrod doesn't sound like it."

Jim frowned at him. "What are you trying to tell me, doctor? I listen pretty well these days."

"I was just thinking that it might pay to talk to Henry Coe before you knock down any more men who testified against you."

"Still a little deaf in that ear."

"Then you're deaf in both. Because Coe can help you, but I'm blessed if I know who else can."

"It's true, Jim," Ann said.

"If I went to a lawyer," said Jim, "he'd say all I can do is sue. So I'd sue. If I won, Wingard could appeal. That's a year or so gone, and who's paying the freight?"

"You could take a job," Ann suggested.

"A job wouldn't pay costs."

"Coe might let you pay his fee later."

"That's one pawn shop where I don't want to be owing money." Jim glanced at the buckskin standing among the trees. "That pony's going to go stiff if I don't get him moving."

Suddenly Ann put her hand on his arm. He saw the fineness of her skin, smelled her cologne, and he was sadly conscious of the delicate structure which supported her and the things she believed in. It was a structure which required always having sufficient money and not permitting unfortunate things to happen to you.

"Don't go out there, Jim," she said. "Tom Elrod and Ed are already waiting for you."

"What about Wingard?" Jim asked.

"I don't know. I don't believe he's left the line camp. Does it matter?"

"Might," Jim said. "Doctor, what did you hear with that thing you were tickling me with? Am I all right for heavy work?"

"Well, providing it isn't too heavy."

"Good," said Jim. He walked over to the horse. In a moment the doctor followed him.

"You know, son," he frowned, "maybe it would be

best all around if you were to try another—climate, say, until things settled down here. You could get your lawsuit started by mail.''

"Don't worry, sir," Jim said. "I'll leave her alone."

"No, no—that's not what—" the doctor began.

But Jim was already riding down the wash toward Three Deuces.

Chapter 9

THE CREEK LED southeast in its shallow wash. Jim jogged along the sand with his new straw sombrero on the back of his head and his new buckskin horse under him. The warm breath of September puffed against his cheek. Suddenly he felt how alone he was, how alone and wonderfully free. He looked around like a man in a new country, his throat tightening with unexpected emotion.

About him everything seemed newly minted for his return. The things he was used to now were a yellow sky pounding the back of his head, white rings of alkali on his clothes where the sweat had dried, looking through superiors rather than at them, being hungry. Potato peeling whisky made in a bucket, fights to the death with a rock and a scrap of iron over nothing but pure despair.

And he felt a desperate pity—pity for the men who were still there. Pity for the young man who had loved this country and been dragged away from it to some idiots with clubs, who wanted to make something less than a man out of him, and had kneaded him like a pan of bread-dough. Jim pitied that young fellow because he had had so much to learn, yet when he had learned it they still weren't satisfied with him. So in despair they had killed him off. It was not Jim Canning they killed, because here he was. He was just a reckless young fellow Jim had known once.

By the creek trail, the ranch buildings were a mile closer than by the wagon road. Where the road crossed Cuero Creek, Jim ducked to pass beneath a log bridge supported with cables. The wash grew deeper, with blocks of stone forming a low cliff on the left and willows fringing its base.

The trail worked among gray boulders and clumps of willow, crossing the creek now and then. The sand and silt held the hoof-prints of two horses which had passed not long ago. Jim's pony turned its head to look back down the trail. He cuffed it alongside the neck to prevent its whickering, held it there, and listened. He could not hear the other horse yet, but it was there, and he had to figure.

After a moment he let the buckskin lope, jumped a log across the trail, and cut into some willows at the foot of the bluff. He took the rope from the saddle and left the horse tied. Carrying rope and rifle, he ran back until he heard the horse coming on the other side of the creek. He laid the carbine in the grass and climbed to a wide ledge overhanging the trail. He shook out a loop in the rope and waited.

Mott Wingard came pushing along through the willows grimly, his stained sombrero down over his eyes. That was how Jim had figured it, knowing Ed and Elrod had gone out earlier. Wingard carried a carbine in his right hand and sat humped in the saddle; a black and white poncho was rolled behind the cantle. Wingard held his rifle above the splashing of the water, brought the pony up the bank, and just as the horse started under Jim it snorted and buck-jumped to the side.

Swearing, Wingard fought the horse. Then his brown, weathered face tilted up and he saw the loop settling toward him. He swung the rifle desperately. But the loop was big and he was in the middle of it. The gun flashed and the enormous, shattering roar shook the rocks. Jim set himself as the pony plunged into the creek. Wingard dropped the gun and tried to take the horse in hand, but just then the rope tightened and Jim kept his balance long enough to see Wingard pulled out of the saddle, to land on his back in the shallow water.

Jim went down the rocks in a scrambling fall, stumbled on the trail and went at the rancher, half falling and half

driving. Wingard, on his knees, was pulling off the rope.
As he freed himself, Jim hit him in the back and both men
sprawled into deeper water. Wingard came up blowing
and swearing and looking for Jim. His sombrero floated
away on the slow current. As Jim waded in, Wingard
threw a wild right-hand punch which thumped Jim's chest
like a drum. Jim caught him around the neck and began
clubbing at his face. He saw blood on his mouth and felt
shaky with excitement as he kept slashing at that distorted
brown face.

Wingard writhed away and brought a wet cobble up
from the water. He lunged in. Jim faded back with his
hands raised, watching as the rancher came toward him.
Wingard's iron-black hair streaked his brow; the blood
from his split lip was dripping onto his shirt. A rock turned
under Jim's boot. Just then Wingard hurled the stone. It
fell through the air where Jim's face had been. Wingard's
hand slapped his holster but it was empty. He groped for
another stone. As he did so, Jim sprawled into him. He hit
him on the side of the head as ne was bringing up the rock,
and Wingard fell aside and stumbled for footing. He
shook his head so that drops of blood sprinkled Jim's shirt.
Jim dug his fist into Wingard's belly, breaking him in the
middle like a stick. Then he dug another up into his jaw.
Wingard floundered back and fell on his side in the long,
shining grass of the bank. Jim pulled him back as he was
sliding into the water. He stared down at him. The
rancher's eyes were half open. Jim felt a little guilty about
jumping him, but what else could he do, with two men
ahead of him and Wingard behind? As if to justify himself
he said hoarsely, ''Do you savvy now that I meant it? I
said you weren't keeping me off my land. By God, I'll
make that stick!''

He searched about until he found the man's carbine. His
revolver was in the creek. Jim threw the rifle into a deep
hole, secured his own, and wént back to his horse.

The principal worry was that Ed Wingard and Tom
Elrod had been snapped alert by Wingard's shot. Yet they

would have been on watch anyway. Jim rode down the canyon, the cliffs piling higher, the sun slanting in on the gray-green willows, the water, the damp sand bars. There was a sharp fragrance of crushed leaves. He passed little bunches of cattle. The canyon made a big clockwise swing and straightened out. Now the right bank began falling back to a meadow. On the other side, the creek hugged the base of the hills.

Jim left his horse in a small side canyon and climbed the hill to a ridge. Breathing deeply, he gazed south. The creek vanished into the hills. The hills ended in a sheer cap rock and he remembered the long sweep of grass and small timber sloping down to the desert and the Rio Grande, fifteen miles away. Below him, less than a half mile from where he stood, a long stone ranch house lay among some pecan trees and a mighty grandfather of a cottonwood. The building had been Wingard's home long ago; but even before he lost the land to Lynn Canning he had not moved, at his wife's insistence, closer to town.

Some pole corrals went with the irregularities of the ground beyond the old ranch house.

Jim could hear the tin-can tolling of a bell from a strip of pasture along the creek, but he could not see Ed or the foreman. He started down the ridge. From directly behind the buildings he inspected the area again. Two horses, ready saddled, were tied near the harness shed. There was a bachelor litter outside the kitchen door. A washboard hung near the door. He studied the flat roofs of the buildings where any capable sentry would post himself, noticing the drifts of brown leaves against the parapets. There was a movement: one of the horses rubbed its nose against its foreleg, then it raised its head to glance at the long gallery of the house.

Ah! Jim thought.

Very carefully he started down the hill. He carried the carbine; yet he was not even sure he could use it. What the hell, he thought, if I carry it they're going to think I mean to use it. And if it's a showdown everybody in sight will be shooting. They'd be shooting anyway, out here with no witnesses. So he kept the gun with him.

A side of antelope hung in a screened cooler behind the kitchen. There was a litter of rusty tin cans under a tree, a pile of stove wood, a water barrel. He stopped behind the house. No dogs, thank God. The cowbell tonked peacefully in the meadow. High overhead buzzards floated like kites. A voice on the porch at the other side of the house said something. Through the windows of the sitting room he could see straight through the house. An *olla* in a rawhide sling was suspended from a roof support of the long front gallery. And now he saw the crown of a Stetson move.

He wet his lips and glanced back up the hill. Wingard might or might not have been able to catch his pony. Jim moved around to the south corner of the building. One of the horses nickered. Tom Elrod spoke quickly and chairs creaked. Spurred boots jarred along the stone floor. Jim slipped back around the corner.

"What do you see?" Elrod called.

"Nothin'." Ed's voice came from across the yard.

"Still say that was a shot we heard a while ago," Elrod contended.

"Maybe. It was four counties away, if it was."

Jim heard Elrod moving about. "Well— Maybeso the horses heard your father comin'. I don't reckon even Canning needed it wrote any plainer than Adams wrote it for him. So he won't likely be coming out."

After a moment Ed replied, "He'll come out."

Jim heard Elrod walking back to the porch. He waited until he heard the chairs scrape as they resumed their watch. Once more he moved around the corner and started working to the front.

Then from the hill, a voice roared like a shotgun, "Look out! It's Canning!"

The gun started in Jim's hand. He heard the chairs crash over. Behind him Mott Wingard was running down the hill, and Jim stood there numbed by shock. In a moment

Elrod and Ed would appear and start chopping at him from ten feet. Jim knew at last he should not have come because he was not ready to use a gun. He set it against the wall, just as Tom Elrod plunged into sight. He spotted Jim, but when he realized Jim had his hands raised he took his rifle by the barrel and came at him, swinging it at his head. There was a strip of court plaster across his lower lip. Jim ducked away and the rifle butt splintered against the wall. He hunched over and charged Elrod. His head butted the ramrod's belly, sliding him down on his back.

Jim jumped Elrod and started for the horses tethered under the big cottonwood, just as Ed came sprinting from the front of the ranch house. A stone caught Jim's foot and he went down so fast his cheekbone cracked against the earth. For a second he was stunned. Distantly someone called, "Get 'im now, boys!"

Then everything jumped into focus—himself lying on his face, Elrod scrambling up to dive on him, and Ed Wingard a few feet behind. He rolled aside, but Elrod landed on him. He squirmed frantically, and then he was on his back and the ramrod was straddling him and slugging at his face. Jim kept rolling his head and Tom Elrod could not land a solid one.

The other men came up. Mott Wingard was wet, dirty and bloody, and he carried no weapons. Ed went to one knee beside them. "Hold his hands!" he panted.

Jim kept hitting at Elrod's face, but the foreman finally caught one wrist and hung onto it. Jim was sobbing with exertion. Ed succeeded in grappling Jim's other hand to the ground. Then he got his knee on Jim's elbow and with both hands opened his fingers and forced them against the earth.

"Dad!" he said commandingly. "Put your foot here."

Jim felt Wingard's boot descend on his fingers. Elrod's weight kept him from moving, Ed's knee pinioned his arm, and the father's boot pressed his hand flat against the earth. Ed took a short hunting knife from his belt and looked down into Jim's face. He was breathing heavily and wore a waxy grin.

"Ed, what the devil are you doing?" Wingard asked sharply.

"Just givin' it back to him!" Ed retorted. "Even-Stephen, that's all."

Jim's gaze turned up to the rancher's face. He looked as if he had been in a barroom brawl. The cut on his mouth was oozing blood again. He frowned at Jim's hand, then peered at Ed, and finally he growled, "Make it quick."

Ed's arm cocked with the knife and Jim's body contorted. There was a cat-snarling instant when he fought them with his teeth, his knees, and his will. He lifted Elrod by arching his back, but Wingard kicked him in the side. Jim shouted as the knife slashed down. He felt it pass through his hand but there was no pain. He tore his right arm loose and slugged at Elrod's face. The ramrod drove at his jaw. Everything took on an iridescent shimmer; something happened very fast and there was a sensation in his hand again and again. At last Elrod's weight was lifted from him. Ed and Wingard stood back. Jim lay flat, looking up at the leafy roof of the tree branches. He kept pulling the air into his lungs but could not fill them. Ed Wingard started to thrust the hunting knife back in the case on his belt, but his father said gruffly, "Give it to me."

He squatted and cleaned the blade with earth. Then he handed it to Ed. The three men walked to the ranch house.

Chapter 10

JIM COULD HEAR their voices. After a time he rolled over on his face and lay like that. He felt as though he had been beaten with ax helves. Pain was beginning to throb in him, and he raised his hand and looked at it. A thick redness was welling through the blood and grit.

He got on his knees. The voices ceased in the ranch house. He pulled out his bandanna and wrapped it about his hand. He wondered if Ed realized he had been hacking at the wrong hand. In the long stone house they were talking again. Dazed, he knelt there. What did they want him to do now? Come to the door and ask for a drink? He glanced at the ranch house. In the window of what had been Jim's room a grim brown face was looking out. Jim's gaze drifted to the carbine standing near the corner of the wall where he had left it. Excitement and rage blazed in his head like a flash. Then Tom Elrod sauntered from the gallery and stood near the corner. Mott Wingard vanished from the window.

So he sat there with that fishhook pain tearing through his hand, thumping his right fist slowly against the ground in agony. In a short time someone banged the door of the ranch house. Boots sauntered toward him. Wingard loomed near by, chewing some food, a chunk of dried venison in his hand.

"I've got a paper there you might like to sign, Canning. Seeing's you've still got a good right hand," he added.

"You go to hell!" Jim said hoarsely.

"I probably shouldn't tell Ed he got the wrong hand," Wingard mentioned.

"As Christ is my witness—!"

"Now, wait! Keep it straight: nobody is your witness. I could have killed you with less effort and risk than we've been to."

Jim rose slowly, while Wingard watched with his rutted features drawn into a curious frown. Blood soaked the bandage over Jim's hand.

"You'd better take care of that hand," Wingard advised "Once it starts to suppurate, you're licked. Might lose it completely. That's what licked Ed. And it's a long walk in."

Jim stared at him. Wingard realized he was not going to answer, and wiped his cut mouth carefully. Then he told him, "Well, she's all yours for a while, mister. We're going in town: *Adiós!*"

As he returned to the house, he picked up the rifle.

Jim walked to the barrel behind the house which collected the run-off of a spring up the hill. Spearmint and sourdock grew in a dense little jungle about the barrel. He knelt to wash in the overflow pool. Presently he heard the horses moving, and Mott Wingard rode back to look at him. "Anything you wanted to say?" he asked.

Jim looked at him fixedly. "I'll be back," he said.

Wingard grunted. "Yes, you came back once before, didn't you? Learn your lesson, Canning: don't show up in Frontera again! Adams will jug you for assault, and you know where that'll end. Send me your address sometime and I'll send the papers for you to sign."

Jim's fist closed. Wingard saw the movement, smiled and said, "Don't get your stove hot again, Jim. Man your size will get burned every time."

Among the things they left him were spilled and crusted food on the stove, trash of every sort, bullet holes in the ceiling, and a bottle of whisky in the kitchen. Jim sat down at the limber-legged kitchen table and drank from the bottle. The whisky pulled its cotton batting over his pain. Placing his elbows on the table, he held the wounded hand up. He could think of nothing but killing them all. The tableau formed in his mind.

He looked uneasily at the bloody wrapping about his hand. The hand was hurting less and bleeding little now. But he thought of all the dirt sealed up within the cuts, and if there was any truth to that yarn about dirt causing wounds to mortify, then he ought to be cleaning it.

He drank some more whisky and walked with lazy, half-drunken strides to the harness shed. Among coils of rope, broken reins and bridles, and lengths of rusty chain, he found some horse medicines. Creosote, turpentine, and bluestone had been said to cure anything, and for full measure there were sweet-oil for colic, hoof ointments, and a few fancier remedies smelling of carbolic acid. He settled on the turpentine, pulled the cork with his teeth, and poured it over his raw palm.

When the pain hit him, he shouted and threw the bottle at the wall. He reeled into the door, held to the edge of it, sank to his knees, and groaned. At last, sweating and weak, he stumbled from the shed.

He returned to finish the whisky. After that he lay on the floor of the kitchen, his hand under his head, and slipped into a stupor of shock and whisky.

Dusk filled the room when he awoke. He lay there until his head began to clear. He was hungry. In a burlap food-locker he discovered jerky, flinty corn dodgers, and some *frijol* beans. He made coffee. Afterward he carried the food to the long porch and gazed across the creek toward the hills folding down into darkness. He ate and sat back with a shaky feeling of convalescence. At last his mind began collecting itself. The talent developed in Huntsville began to come out—that dogged ability to take a whipping without being drawn out of position.

No, he decided, he was not ready to strap on his guns and call himself the Huntsville Kid. Wingard was the man who would mint the profits of that foolishness. For this

Hawk Adams—unless he shattered under fire like a lamp chimney—would clip the wings of a fledgling gunhawk before he pecked his way out of his shell. Jim stood at the mouth of that dark alley of retaliation in which he smelled catastrophe and decided not to enter it.

In disgust he tossed his tin cup to the floor. So what he had to have was a lawyer. Every man in Huntsville could tell you out of the corner of his mouth about some lawyer he was going to kill. Obviously they were all there because a lawyer somewhere had tripped over his tongue.

And how was he going to pay for a lawyer? Take a job, Ann had suggested. Wingard's lease money would pay for the court fight. But Wingard was four months behind right now; and he was not the man to provide bullets for a gun at his head.

There was only one answer to it. It had been in his mind all along like a mouse in the attic: see Henry Coe.

He pictured Coe grinning to himself in his red-faced, shut-lipped way as if he had a mouthful of buckshot he did not want to spill. *Sign here, Jim. Be glad to help—for half of your ranch.*

There were a lot of people in Frontera about whom he was absolutely sure: the Wingards, Elrod, Hawk Adams. But there was still some mystery about Judge Coe. He was the bottle labeled *Poison*, which sometimes smelled, however, like a very good bourbon.

Chapter 11

THOUGH THE JUDGE was not given to premonitions, he slept little the night after Jim Canning came home. First he was too warm, then he was too cold. Just as he would doze off, a dog would bark and cue a town-wide glee club. Suddenly he would recollect something he had forgotten to take care of, and with a groan he would tramp around the bedroom hunting a pencil until his wife sighed in exasperation, "Henry, *will* you settle down? It must be after twelve!"

"It's a quarter to two," Coe muttered, snapping shut the lid of his hunting watch.

"Drink some warm milk, dear," Mrs. Coe advised, herself almost asleep again.

"Do you think I'm a child?" Coe snapped.

Late the next morning Mott Wingard, his son, and Tom Elrod rode into town. Coe saw this from his window. They went to the Big Corner Saloon, at the end of the block, and later rode south, probably to Hammond's feed barn. Coe hastened to the saloon to find out what was going on. As a man of standing, he had only to take a place at his usual table, and the information would shortly arrive. Ira Moore brought his noontime drink over. The banker had forgotten to remove his paper sleeve-protectors before hurrying from the bank. His thin brown face drew down sourly.

"God!" he said. "Some people! And here I was almost

feeling sorry for Canning!''

Coe calmly raised his whisky glass. "What's he done?"

"Bulldogged Mott Wingard into the creek, and tackled Tom Elrod and Ed with a carbine! Then Wingard got in on it and there was a hell of a row."

"Couldn't have been too bad," said Coe. "They rode in straight up and down in the saddle." He sipped the liquor, set the glass down, and since Moore was not getting to it, asked, "How'd Jim come out?"

"They whipped his backsides all over Three Deuces, I gather."

Something as sharp as the whisky found a galled place in Henry Coe's mind. "At least that's how they're telling it," he rapped.

Moore's pale, deep-set eyes glanced up. "Why not? He pulled the same damn fool stunt before."

"With the same witnesses. Let's hope, Ira, that these veteran tale-bearers are good men and true."

"I've always thought of Mott Wingard as a fairly substantial man," said the banker dryly.

Coe shot him a scowl. "Don't give me that! The size of a man's bank account has no visible effect on his ability to tell the truth. I don't know why," he said slowly, "but I feel guilty as hell about Jim."

"Why should you? If you hadn't heard his trial, somebody else would have. Somebody who might have given him ten years."

Leaning back, the judge removed his spectacles and tapped a silver bow against his teeth. "Want to know where it really started? It started when a gambler hit town one night when Mott Wingard was drinking too much. Pretty soon he was betting too much. Gambling was this man's business and he was glad to take Wingard's money. Wingard kept thinking he could double-or-nothing himself out of his troubles. At least give Canning's father credit for allowing him every chance to win back what he'd lost."

"Great sacrifice," murmured Moore.

"It would have been if he'd lost!" snapped Coe. "That's the attitude that's made it tough for Jim all these years. The idea that it was unfair for a gambler to take land from a big man like Mott Wingard! Why, it could happen to anyone. You're damn right it could! But from that day on, how much chance has anybody given Jim to grow up like other Frontera boys?"

Moore's lips hardened, but he did not reply. Coe finished his drink, replaced his spectacles, and rose.

"Anyway, that's how it looks to me. But I expect I've gotten into a bad habit of wanting to hear both sides."

As he was leaving the saloon, a cowboy came in, slapped his hands on the bar, and announced breathlessly, "Mott Wingard's just signed a warrant for Canning's arrest!"

"What for?" asked the judge quickly.

"Assault with a deadly weapon!" the puncher said.

The judge hurried to his office. He was cold with anger. For two hours he labored grimly over some law books. He could almost reconstruct, now, what had happened: They had given Jim a bad whipping, one that ought to make it clear to him where he stood. But to make certain he did not return, Wingard was turning him over to Adams. Back to Huntsville: that was what it meant. Painstakingly, Coe reviewed the statutes on assault. There were so many loopholes that nearly any attorney should be able to make a case in either direction.

At six he went home to dinner. He returned at seven, lighted the lamps and lay on the floor with a book under his head to rest and think.

Did the pious fools in this town know they were under the gun as well as Jim Canning? For if Jim were beaten, it would be by muscle and gun and money: jungle law. Let that happen to one man and what protection did the rest have? Coe's law books would become cowhide headrests.

Coe got off the floor with a grunt and tramped downstairs. Under the big, dark shade trees he walked up the block to jail.

At his roll-top desk, Marshal Adams was eating dinner. He glanced up, sucking a tooth. It was hot in the office. Insects darted at the lamp atop Adams's roll-top desk. Under the cone of light his olive skin looked oily. A revolver lay on the desk not far from his hand.

"Take a seat, judge," said the marshal. "Big doin's for our little town, eh?"

Coe stood clenching his fists. "Not unless we make them big."

"Your Honor, you plumb mystify me sometimes!" said Adams.

"I'll make it less mysterious: Canning and the Wingards had a fight. Wingard got here first and made a complaint. Does that make him right?"

Mildly, Adams said, "Nobody said he was."

"Then remember that when you arrest Canning."

"When I arrest Canning," replied the marshal, "it'll be between him and me and nobody else. Suppose *you* remember *that*. I told him not to pack a gun, and he went right out and borrowed one. So I know he's armed. If it's all the same to you, I'll take due precautions when I arrest him."

"If due precautions mean shooting him—" Coe was light-headed with rage and frustration. He watched Adams slap a mosquito on his hairy wrist.

"If I shoot him," said Adams slowly, "it'll just be up to the county to bury him. That what you were fixing to say?"

Turning, Coe left the office and slammed the mosquito-netted door. *I'll start a recall movement!* he thought bitterly. Recall for what? For doing such a good job people hated him? Recall for filling the potholes in Houston Street, repairing rotten boardwalks, cracking down on smuggling?

He marched back upstairs, trying to recall laws with

which he might crack a seam in Adams's tough armor. He opened the door. His stomach dropped as he saw the man sitting at his desk.

"Well—well, I'll be bound!" he stammered.

Jim Canning smiled sadly and said, "I reckon I already have been, judge. Bound and beat. Thought maybe you and I could have that talk now."

Coe hurried to draw the shades.

When he saw Jim's hand, he shivered. "Neeley'd better see that damned quick."

Jim moved to the visitor's seat and the judge sat at the desk, feeling guilty and rattled.

"Jim," the judge said, "tell me about yourself. How are you? I mean aside from what's just happened. I suppose I'm thinking about what that cross breeding of a madhouse and a pigpen has done to you."

Jim leaned back and gazed at the shadowy ceiling. "Just before my father died he said something I'll never forget. He'd had his worst spell, and nothing eased it for him. 'Jim,' he said, 'I've been in one of those little rooms we aren't supposed to know about.' I reckon you can't tell a man about that little room I've been in either. But if you ever get there, judge, you'll know why I didn't want to shake hands with you the other day."

Coe viewed his sad and battered face with an inner shrinking. He caught completely the feeling of a man beaten and alone. He closed his eyes and began nodding. "I know, Jim. I know. Jim," he asked, "what was the honest-to-God truth about your fight with Ed Wingard? What ailed Ed to draw that gun?"

He saw Jim's hesitation. "He was sore because I cut out some of his old man's fence. Wingard had moved it two hundred yards into our land after my father died. It ran right across the base of a bluff where our cattle trailed to the creek, so they couldn't get to the water. I cut it, and some of our old graze bulls got in with Wingard's fancy cows."

Coe blinked in his nearsighted manner. He leaned

across the desk to adjust the wick of the lamp. "And you didn't hooraw Ed a little? Didn't make an ass of him?"

Again Jim seemed to select the best way of saying something. "Sure, we had some words."

"Tell you what I always figured happened. Ed and Elrod were fixing that fence when you came along. You cut it, as they testified. You kept on cutting while Ed worked himself into a lather. And you kept joshing him until probably even Elrod was laughing at the boy. As everybody but Mott Wingard knows, Ed isn't the stablest man in this county."

"Why would I do that?" Jim frowned.

"So he'd try something foolish and you could whip the tar out of him. You could have waited till they left and then cut the fence. But you were dying to rub his nose in the dirt. Maybe you had reason to dislike him. But the way I felt, you took advantage of him. That's why I didn't take your case. I felt you should have picked on somebody your own size—say, his father."

After a while Jim said slowly, "Maybe you're right. I guess I was dying to get my hands on Ed. But he was such a damned fool somebody would have cleaned his plow sooner or later. And it was a way I could get at his old man."

"Then you should have gone after his old man. Or was he too big for you?"

Jim could see it, now that Coe had pulled off the wrappings. "Maybe that was it, judge. Understand me, though: I'd take on Wingard in a fair scrap any time. But you know where that would have landed me. Tangling with the man who runs the town, the county, and the bank. Ed was the closest I could get to the big one, and I guess I couldn't pass up the chance."

Coe sat back. "Well, that's why I felt you had some licks coming. In a way, Ed was just a child."

Jim glanced at the bloody bandage on his hand. "But he's getting to be a pretty unruly child, judge."

Coe winced. "What happened?"

"They teamed up. It was Ed's idea to use a knife on my hand."

Coe grunted. "My God!" Then he said angrily, "He *is* getting to be a big boy, isn't he? Just about the right size for Huntsville, I'm thinking."

Chapter 12

"THE FIRST JUMP," the judge told Jim, "is to get Neeley up here to see that hand. Adams is looking for you, so you'd better stay put. How'd you get in?"

"I caught my horse up the line. Wingard had dumped my saddle and gear in the creek. There was a paper in it I wanted you to look over. But the ink's run now."

Coe was pulling on his coat. "You mean that lease? Just trash. It's on file at the courthouse, so I've seen it. It was improperly executed because you didn't have your signature witnessed."

Canning was on his feet now, looking excited. "Then why can't I just pitch them off?"

"Because first you've got to whip them in court. But that will take money. Got any?"

Jim shook his head. "When I think of money, I think of cattle. Buy low, sell high—that's all I know about finance. But they'd have to be pretty sorry cattle before I could buy them without cash. No, wait," he said. "What about those feed-lot wonders of Neeley's? Reckon I could get them on consignment?"

"Bright boy, Jim," Coe smiled. "But where would you sell them if you could?"

Jim sat with his elbows resting on his knees. "Know a Mexican named Ámador?"

"Mario? Sure. And I knew his family when I was a lawyer in Chihuahua City."

"Well, he was trying to sell me some horses the first

day I was here. Now I'm wondering if I could sell him some cattle instead. What about him buying them and reselling to one of the armies across the line?"

Coe laughed. "Jim, given any chance at all you'll horsetrade Wingard right into the poorhouse. You've just unwrapped the present I put under your Christmas tree when I heard you were coming home. Mario came up last month looking for beef to buy. But Adams was watching him too close so I advised him to lay low. When I got word that you were getting out, I thought that was practically providential. Since the cattle are already out in your end of the valley, you could move them out without Adams ever knowing about it. So Mario's been counting the days till you got here."

"How and when do I start?"

"You start by having a drink with Mario at the cantina in the morning. He'll be ready to travel. But right now all you can do is sit still while I go for Neeley."

After the judge had left, it seemed to Jim that something intangible but important had gone with him. Now the shadows which had given character to the room seemed like concealing draperies hung in the corners. Through the oiled flooring rose a blunted clatter of china and silver from the hotel dining room. Now that it was too late to matter, Jim wondered whether the marshal had had anyone watching the livery stable. Men like Felipillo Vasquez thought such work honorable and distinguished.

Downstairs, the door opened again and he listened. At least two men were mounting the stairs; yet it seemed too early for Coe to be returning. One of the men wore spurs, so he could be neither Coe nor the doctor. Jim glanced about the room. There was no other door, and no closet in which to hide. He sat at the desk until the men reached the landing. A man said a word, there was a hesitation, and then the knob turned and the door opened quickly. But no one entered.

"We know you're in there, Canning," said the marshal's voice.

Jim said, "Well, don't let it bother you."

"It ain't bothering me," said Adams. "I just wanted the judge to have a chance to get out of line."

"He's not here. Come on in."

"No. You come out."

There was no hope of stalling until the judge returned. Adams would turn delay into an excuse to fire. He might fire anyway. In that case, Jim thought it would be better to take a bullet standing than sitting. He walked to the doorway, hesitated, and went on into the gloom of the landing. Adams was at the top of the stairs, his Colt gleaming darkly. He made his cigar glow and his pocked face was ruddily lighted. Another man slid in behind Jim and shoved a revolver into his back.

Mott Wingard said harshly, "Man, you are a slow learner. Maybe the marshal and I can teach you what I couldn't teach you alone."

"You just know I can, and without anybody's help, either," said Adams. "Teachin' bad boys is the best thing I do." He strolled past Jim into the office, glanced about, and dropped the cigar on the floor as he came out.

"So far," Jim told him, "you haven't said what you're arresting me for."

"Same as before, boy: assault with intent. Well, time's wasting. Let's go."

When the judge returned with the doctor, he found the room empty and the cigar in the middle of the floor. He picked up the cigar and threw it out the door as if it were the marshal himself. He strode out and met Neeley on the stairs. "Patient's been moved," he said. "Let's get over to the jail."

At the jail, men were standing on the walk and in the road. Coe pushed through the crowd and looked down at the men in the small room. Manacled, Jim sat in a corner behind the roll-top desk, where Adams, his sleeves rolled, was taking a statement of facts from Mott Wingard. Wingard was watching Adams's big, calm hand move over the paper. The marshal's white linen shirt adhered to his perspiring shoulders. Tom Elrod was rolling a cigarette, and Ed Wingard was inspecting the marshal's case of curios. Coe saw him bite a knuckle as if to draw a splinter from it.

"If you can find room," the judge said, "Doctor Neeley and I would like to come in."

Adams looked up, leaned back, and said loudly to the room at large, "All right—all of you tramps get out of here. I won't tell you again."

The men went obediently from the room, and Coe and the doctor entered. Marshal Adams drawled, "Rushing the season, ain't you, judge? First the questions, then the lawyers and doctors."

"We'll try not to get underfoot," the judge assured him.

Adams frowned and resumed his writing. Coe lighted a cigar and when it was drawing he laid it on Adams's paper. Adams removed it with an oath. "Now, what in hell—"

"There's enough rum in those cigars of yours to spike a punch," the judge told him. "Hereafter I'll ask you not to leave them on my rug. Under what section is this man being booked?"

"The main caper as far as I'm concerned," Adams said, "is breaking parole."

"In what way?"

"Are you tryin' this case, judge, or just inquisitive?"

"I'm curious about the same thing happening twice with the same witnesses—except that this time Canning seems to be the victim instead of the criminal."

Mott Wingard's scarred and heavy features locked into a scowl. "Canning jumped me in Cuero Canyon. Later he tried to bushwhack my son and Tom Elrod. You can read it in the affidavit, if you're interested."

"I thought I might," Coe said, taking the paper from the desk.

Adams's report was ungrammatical, but through his

pen had flowed as black a tar as a parolee could be painted with. Coe cleared his throat.

"This statement, *'tried to kill me, my son, Ed, and my foreman, Tom Elrod, by ambushing us with a rifle.'* Were any shots fired by Canning?"

Wingard said crisply, "Yes."

"Where's the gun?" asked Coe. Then seeing the Henry lying on the desk, he put his finger in the muzzle, twisted it out and looked at it. It was clean.

"I cleaned it before we came in," Wingard said.

Coe shrugged. "Evidence which has been tampered with is no longer evidence."

"The fact that he was carrying it," rapped Adams, "is all the evidence I need that Canning broke parole! I told him not to buy a gun, and he set right out and done it anyway."

"No, sir," declared Jim. "It was borrowed."

"Borrowed or bought—" began the marshal angrily.

"Look here," Coe said, "I can produce witnesses that your specific instructions to this man did *not* include borrowing a gun! In that case, jailing him would constitute false arrest!"

Adams rose, planted his fists on the desk, and leaned toward him. Oil gleamed on the man's tan skin; a sharp stubble darkened his jaws. "You can smart talk all the chuckleheads you want to, Your Honor," he said, "but don't try to pull it on this 'coon. I'll slap you in a cell as quick as I'd drop a hot rock. Heard about interfering with an officer of the law, ain't you?"

"Rubbish," said Coe. But looking into the flinty slits of the marshal's eyes, he was uneasy. He thought of Jim alone with him for a night and felt a chill.

"You better clear out o' here," Adams decided.

"You listen to me—" began Coe.

Adams came around the desk and gripped his arm. He smelled of bay rum and perspiration. "Are you going to get out or am I going to pitch you out?"

A woman's voice intruded. "May I come in?"

Coe glanced around and saw Ann on the threshold. Doctor Neeley hurried to take her arm and lead her out, but she shook her head and came into the room. The doctor said something in a harsh tone, but she only glanced at him with a frown and said, "No, father—you run on, if you like. I'll come as soon as I can."

Adams regarded her without pleasure. "I know I'm intruding," Ann said, "but I've just remembered something very important. I was sure you'd want to know about it, since it concerns Jim Canning."

"Oh, I'm always interested in Canning," Adams assured her. "Why don't you come around in the morning and tell me all about it?"

"Actually it isn't my story to tell. It's my father's. Dad, what was it Ed said to us when we were driving to the ranch?"

Neeley locked his mouth tightly and gazed in anger at his daughter. "About what?" he replied finally.

"Oh, you remember. About his hand—"

Wingard interrupted sharply. "I thought doctors generally kept such information to themselves."

Neeley bridled. "I'm aware of the code, sir. However, I'm at a loss to know what Hippocrates would say about patients who ask a physician how to go about *causing* a certain type of injury."

"Sure enough? Little Ed ask that?" the marshal chuckled.

Neeley hesitated. "Well, you see, he appeared at first to be interested in exactly why his own hand had withered. Then he said that unless Jim Canning were careful, he'd wind up with a hand like his own. And then he said he was going out to Canning's ranch to wait for him."

"And afterward," Ann added, "father said that he was beginning to think they'd sent the wrong man to prison."

Ed Wingard was walking quickly toward her. Seizing her by the shoulders, he turned her to face him. "That's not what I said! I just asked— well, if you had a hand like mine—" He held the wizened little hand in the air, staring fiercely at Jim, then at the marshal, then at the doctor. Suddenly he turned to seize the girl by the shoulders again, but the marshal dragged him back and jammed him into a corner.

"Wait a minute, little fella," he said. "Get those hackles down. Hawk'll have to put a ring in your nose—"

Mott Wingard whipped Adams around and hit him on the jaw. There was a flat smack of bone and flesh. Adams went back against the wall and Ed darted away. Coe saw Adams's eyes waver. Then the marshal shook his head, and his hand flashed to his holster in a motion as fast as the flick of the inner eyelid of a bird. But the holster was empty. He squeezed the thick leather, staring at Wingard. The gun lay on his desk, where, apparently, he had laid it while manacling Jim.

"How'd you ever get the name of Hawk?" Wingard baited him.

Adams spat on his hand and rocked forward. Coe hurried to step between the men. "Just a minute, marshal. You and the County of Socorro, Texas, are running right close to a parting of the ways when you start roughing up citizens because they get a bit carried away."

"Carried away! By God, they'll carry *him* away!"

"I warn you," Coe threatened. "I'll convene a grand jury tonight."

"Are you crazy? You saw him slug me."

"What did you expect—muscling the man's son around that way?"

Adams turned to Ann. "Will you tell him *why* I was muscling the man's son around? He laid his dirty hands on you, didn't he?"

Ann looked helplessly from the judge to the marshal. "You know, marshal, I really didn't call for help."

Adams was still seething as his fingers turned a big silver ring on his hand. After a moment he walked to his desk. "Are you going to make charges against anybody?" he asked Jim.

"Depends."

"How about you?" Adams asked Mott Wingard.

Wingard turned his gaze on Jim. For a while he was silent, then a muscle twitched in the lower lid of one eye, and Jim discerned in the leathery face the violence now under control.

"Not in the way you mean," Mott said finally.

"Better spell that out," Adams suggested. "I'm just an old cow-country marshal, you know."

"I mean I won't come crying to you with my troubles any more. I hope I haven't been a nuisance to you, marshal. I know you must be busy with drunks and all. But the fact is that in this country things haven't changed at all: a man that wants something done still has to do it himself."

"What do you want done?" asked Adams mockingly.

"I want to be able to ride my own land without being waylaid. If you can't promise me that, I'll make Canning a promise. That I'll meet him with a rifle the next time he comes calling."

"Oh, I'll stay off *your* land," Jim said. "But just don't forget that when you talk about Deuces, you're talking about mine."

Adams tossed some keys to a man standing near Jim. He ran a sour glance about the office. "Now, you men listen to me and tell your friends: next man that takes a cut at Hawk will go to bed with a bullet in his liver. I see some of you packin' guns. Now, I take that to mean you know how to defend yourselves, so don't look like you're sweatin' to lag pennies with the experts, or you may be asked to. Canning, it would be a good idea if you was to report to me every day for a while. Wingard," he added, "you and your little yella wolf may have business with me yet. I kinda think you will."

"We won't be hard to find."

"Not if you ever make a fist where I can see it, you won't. Just turn over the first headstone on the left, and there you'll be."

The Wingards and Elrod left. Doctor Neeley spoke to

Jim without enthusiasm. "You'd better come up to my office. I can take care of your hand better there."

"All right," Jim said.

"Thank you, marshal," said Ann, "for all you've done."

"Oh, it's nothing," said the marshal, "compared to what I'm going to do."

Chapter 13

IT WAS LATE when the doctor finished with Jim's hand. By the time he had stretched the last strip of court plaster, Jim was soaked with perspiration. Neeley handed him two bottles of medicine.

"If you're inclined to think my orders are hard to follow," he said, "remember Ed Wingard. An injury like this can go either way. You'll be wise to use that hand as little as necessary."

"Right," Jim said. As the doctor rose from his desk he spoke quickly, "I don't need an answer to this now, sir. But I'm looking for some cattle on consignment."

"I don't think you'd want mine on any basis, would you?"

"These would be for quick butchering," Jim said. "They'd do."

Neeley frowned. "It seems to me I've done you one favor already tonight, James."

"Then you might say I'm doing you one. How are you going to sell cattle like that to a regular buyer?"

"I don't know, James. But I do know I can't take another risk on them. It would have to be cash, at nine dollars."

"I'll give you eleven, on consignment," Jim said quickly.

Neeley's hand was on the door. He pondered. "Very well. When do you want them?"

"Tomorrow," said Jim. "I ought to be back with the

money in four days.''

''All right. I'll look at your hand again at that time. Good night.''

During all this time he had not looked Jim in the face.

The cold night air braced Jim as he left the big, dark house. He stopped to breathe deeply and exhale the last of Neeley's iodoform from his lungs. Standing there, he heard a window grate cautiously. From his right, Ann whispered, ''Jim?''

Jim walked carefully down the narrow strip of devil grass which lapped up to the house. In the long, dark frame of a window he found her, kneeling on the floor with her arms resting on the sill. A gown of dotted material was buttoned to her throat and her dark hair hung in two braids. Her hands were folded on the sill. Jim put his hands over them.

''Well,'' Ann said, with a little laugh.

He held her hand firmly. ''Surprised?'' he asked. ''You didn't think I'd noticed you?''

''Just nicely surprised,'' she said.

''You do everything nicely,'' he said. ''You write nice letters, you get nicely surprised—you even visit jails nicely.''

''Well, I suppose I'm just a nice dull girl,'' she smiled. She looked pleased, and a little nervous. Sobering, she asked, ''What did father say about your hand?''

''He said *quién sabe,* and keep out of fights. I get that *quién sabe* all right, but how am I going to keep out of fights? The only way is to drift.''

''And you aren't going to do that. Jim,'' she said, ''I had the feeling tonight that everything has started to work out.''

Jim smiled. ''You talk the most nonsense I ever heard.''

''No, it's the truth. You'll probably be back on your own land in a month.''

''Put me down for a carload of that,'' Jim told her.

''Be serious, Jim.''

Down the line of windows a voice said, "Did you call me, Ann?"

Ann put her finger over her lips. Turning, she called toward her door, "I just said good night, father."

"Oh— Good night, dear."

A window opened, Jim heard someone breathing deeply and exhaling mightily into the night. Then the old man yawned and rawhide bed springs creaked.

"I eavesdropped a little," Ann said. "I heard you ask him something about our cattle."

He told her about his idea and the arrangements Coe had made with Ámador. "It was kind of *quién sabe* about those cattle of the doctor's, too, but he finally said I could have them on consignment. Of course I'm paying risk prices."

"Still, you're in business," she said. Her face was close. As he looked at her she became grave and expectant, as if she heard him saying the things he was only thinking. He leaned close and kissed her.

She pulled away from him—less to end the kiss than to look at him. She was smiling faintly.

"It wouldn't do at all for you to go away, Jim," she said. "No man I ever met would seem like much now."

"You don't even know me, Ann. In a way we've just met."

"I know you better than you know yourself. I don't think I'm wrong about you."

"Can you tell when a man is falling in love with you?"

Her fingertips touched the stubble on his face. "Oh, that's instinctive."

"Everything about you is instinctive. You know I'm going to be a cattle king, you know I won't break my parole—you know I love you. You're at least two feet off the ground."

"But it's lovely up here."

Why didn't I leave her alone? he was thinking. She had her instincts; but he had his premonitions. To stay alive here, with guns cocking all over town, and to wear anything like pride—those tricks would be very neat ones.

Doctor Neeley returned to his bed with feelings of guilt and disquiet. He had known something was going on, and he was naturally curious to know how much. So he had walked barefoot over the cold tiles to his daughter's door to listen. At last he heard the gate creak and went to bed.

I don't think I'm unreasonable, he thought unhappily. I want to be fair to them. But what kind of life could she have with an ex-convict? Assuming her ex-convict lived through his little war. Children would come; and a man whose only trade was cattle, but had no ranch, scarcely qualified as a provider.

She was still so young. Scarcely twenty. And how could a person who was a child only three or four years ago be considered truly adult? And now his wife was gone, his three older children had married and moved away. When Ann married he would be entirely alone. If only she stays in Frontera . . .

Next morning Mott Wingard called on the doctor.

The doctor took him into his office. He was firm and cool. But in a way he was apprehensive of the rancher, of his hard and humorless directness. Wingard sat down, crossed his legs and hung his hat on his boot toe.

"Doc, I want to know about that remark you and your daughter quoted Ed as making. Is that actually what he said?"

"Substantially. At first I thought he was merely curious about his own deformity. Then I got the feeling there was something else."

The rancher glanced up, his eyes keen in his weathered, vigorous face. "Naturally, being his father, I choose to think you're wrong."

Neeley shrugged. "Apparently it doesn't matter, unless young Canning chooses to sue for damages. Was there anything else?"

"I heard this morning he'd bought your cattle," the

cattleman mentioned, leaning back in the chair.

Standing behind his desk, Neeley tapped it with his fingertips. "Where did you hear this?"

Wingard smiled. "I really deduced it. Do you know that Mexican, Ámador, who's been loafing around town? Well, he's buying cattle for a shirt-tail army down in Chihuahua. Ámador and Canning have a cattle deal on, and I just guessed that nobody but you would be willing to sell to him on the terms he must be asking."

Resentful of the rancher's prying, Neeley retorted, "It could be for cash, couldn't it?"

"Where would Canning get cash?"

"Suppose I have sold him my cattle?" returned the doctor. "It's between Canning and me, isn't it?"

Wingard rose. "Entirely. But if you really want a jailbird for a son-in-law, you're going about it right. The sooner Canning knows he's whipped, the sooner he'll pull out. The longer he stays, the surer you are of being the man who stands up when the preacher asks, 'Who giveth this woman to this ex-convict?' "

He walked to the door. Neeley hated himself for not having the courage to tell Wingard to keep out of his affairs. Even more, he was ashamed of being about to pick up and use against Jim the weapon Wingard had pointed out to him. Wingard seemed to sense his change.

"It wouldn't have to be a flat turn-down," he pointed out. "No one could blame you for asking cash for those cattle. Believe me, if you send them off with two fly-by-nights like those, you'll be giving them away!"

After the rancher left, Neeley wrote a note to Jim Canning and sent a Mexican boy to find him and deliver it.

Chapter 14

THAT MORNING JIM walked down to Hammond's feed barn to close the deal for the buckskin. The horse was not in the stall where Hammond had put it, and he walked back to where the old man was trimming the hoofs of a pony. Horse did not look up.

"See anything of a jack-legged buckskin?" Jim asked at last.

Hammond bent over the hoof locked between his knees. "He's back yonder. Gave him quite a workout, didn't you?"

"Ran plumb out of time, Horse. But I blanketed him when I came in."

"Uh-huh. He rolled in that blanket and tore hell out of it."

Jim rubbed his nose, frowning at the stableman. "What's the charge?"

"No charge. Only cool him out, next time. How's the hand?"

"First hand I've ever had I could cover my eyes with and still see daylight. Got advantages, you see."

"I was mighty sorry to hear about it. Say, did you know that horse threw a shoe yesterday?"

"Never noticed."

"Dang right he did. Threw a shoe and chipped hell out of his hoof. I can't see myself putting a shoe on that hoof for two weeks."

"Hard luck," said Jim. "Maybe I'd better look for something else, eh?"

"I think."

"Is Wingard paying you to renege, or did he just throw a scare into you?" asked Jim.

Hammond scowled. "That ain't it, Jimmy. I just meant— Well, a bad hoof like that—"

Jim counted out some coins. "Four dollars pay for the blanket? I'll pay for the saddle when I sell these cows."

"Oh, now, look here—"

"If that's Wingard's horse," said Jim, "do me a favor and hack off the rest of that hoof."

It was not yet ten, but Jim walked up to Vasquez's cantina. He pushed at the knee-length doors and went in. The saloon had the sound, sensible architecture of a chicken house—the raw adobe walls—very practical—whitewashed partitions, and an easily maintained dirt floor. It had acquired the fine, gamy smell of a hen house, too, since old Vasquez retired and Felipillo and his guitar took over. Felipillo smiled, nodded, and went on practicing chords. It was a smile of courteous dislike.

Back in the perpetual dusk of a corner Jim saw the man, Mario, at his table. Seeing Jim, Mario came quickly to meet him. He was very clean and sober this time, and gave Jim the Mexican *abrazo* instead of a handshake. He was wearing a short buckskin jacket edged with white leather gray with washing, and tight buckskin pants with wrinkled cowhide leggings coming above the knees.

"Coffee, *chamaco*," Mario signaled Felipillo.

"I see you're ready to travel," Jim commented. "When did you talk to the judge?"

"Last night. Did you negotiate with the doctor?"

"He'll sell. He says there's a hundred and sixty-eight cows. Where do we take them?"

"Just to the border and across. Only about fifteen miles."

"Any cash involved?"

"Thirteen dollars a head."

"Payable when?"

"When you come back." Mario leaned forward and lowered his voice. "The money is in a joint account with Judge Coe. I signed a draft this morning. The judge will sign also and hand you the draft. Very quick and clean, you see." He smiled.

Like a bullet, thought Jim.

They were silent while Felipillo placed two mugs of cold, creosote-dark coffee on the table. "We leave when?" Mario asked.

"You can go any time. I'll round up some food and a horse. You wouldn't want to pay for those cattle in advance?" he asked seriously.

Mario raised one shoulder and spread his hands, wryly smiling. "Not that I haven't faith—"

"That's right," Jim said. "Bad business practice. There was a saddle I wanted to pay for."

The slatted doors swung rustily. Mario, who was facing the front, tapped the table warningly. Jim heard slow, spurred strides coming down the room. Heard them pause and a man humming softly. The boots went to the counter and Hawk Adams's voice said, "Gimme a glass of something that ain't got flies in it, Felipillo."

"Sure, *Señor Gavilán!*"

Gavilán meant hawk. It probably flattered the marshal. Jim sat still, squeezing the cup hard with both hands. *"He's like a horse,"* Hammond had said. *"He can strike you from any angle."*

He heard Adams blow out his breath and drop a coin in Felipillo's guitar. "That'll do till somebody invents whisky, I reckon."

He sauntered to Jim's table and stood gazing down at the men. Jim glanced up. "I'd say you were in pretty bad company for a jailbird,'' said the marshal.

"I asked the mayor to join me," Jim said, "but he couldn't make it."

"Keep talkin'," said Adams. "You'll get it."

He went out.

"Will he make trouble?" asked Mario tensely.

"A man can still buy cattle, even in Frontera. But I've got a feeling a law may be passed against it any time. *Bueno*," he said, rising. "I'll see you at Neeley's camp, probably this side of sundown."

At the door he stopped to run a coin across the strings of the Mexican's guitar. "*Amigo*," he asked, "how come you to have all the tequila you want and nobody else has any?"

"Who knows? Maybe I import it, eh?"

"Maybe Hawk looks the other way. Tell him what you just heard us talking about and maybe he'll let you put in a line of fried cactus worms in oil. Very tasty with smuggled tequila." He dropped the coin into the instrument.

He made up his mind to get the business of reporting to the marshal over with. If he did not check in, Adams would come looking for him. As he walked up the block, a Mexican boy ran across the street to hand him an envelope. Then without a word he darted away.

Jim opened it. Hard-eyed, he read the doctor's embarrassed attempt to squirm out of their deal. —*And in all fairness to myself I can see no other way than to ask you to pay cash for the cattle*.

Jim slipped the letter into his hip pocket and walked on. In poker, it was called freeze-out. Even in poker, it was usually considered unworthy. Cash— What cash?

Adams's appaloosa was tied to the rack before the jail. Jim entered. He stopped with a frown. At his desk, the marshal was doing something to his left arm. He had a basin of water on the floor, a rag in it, and his sleeve was rolled to the shoulder. In the white flesh of his biceps Jim could see a small hole, like an eye with a rim of red flesh around it.

Adams's eyes raised with lazy dislike. "Ever think of knocking at doors, cowboy?"

"Well—not in a place like—" Jim began.

"A place like what?"

"Well, sort of public—like a store."

"All you'll ever buy in this store is trouble. Go out and try it again."

Jim went out, knocked, and waited a full minute with the level of irritation rising in him before Adams growled, "Come in."

Jim stood behind the desk, watching the marshal draw out an oakum string which had been laced through the wound in his arm. He had tied a fresh piece of string to the underside, and having pulled it through, cut off the old one and dropped it in the basin.

He smiled at Jim. "Doctor's orders. Reckon bullet holes are old stuff to a loose-triggered child like you, eh?"

Jim watched him begin to wrap the arm. "You notice it's in my left," Adams said. "So don't get overconfident. What do you want?"

"You told me to check in."

"That's so. Quite an evening we had. I guess old Hawk drew to a busted flush that time, eh?"

"It looked like keno all around."

"That's the way to talk," Adams grinned. "Stay out of trouble that way. Empty that basin in the street, will you?"

Jim emptied the basin with its ugly bit of string. Just like old times in Huntsville. *Any you guys feel like makin' trouble? What's the matter, skinny, ain't you the toughest knife fighter in Texas?*

He returned and set the basin on the floor. "No, on the cabinet," said Adams. Jim placed it there and turned.

Adams gazed at him with one eyebrow quirked as he rolled down his sleeve. "What are you doing—hiding behind the desk?"

"Just cautious, marshal."

"Get over that. You wouldn't last a week in tough country, all nerved up thataway."

"I've been through some pretty tough country already this week," said Jim.

"Week ain't gone yet, either," chuckled Adams.

He had planned to visit the bank, more or less as a gesture. If Moore turned him down, he could live on hardtack and *panola* until he had some money. But Neeley had given the screw a vicious turn. Now he *must* have money. As he turned the corner a big man in a brown canvas coat, dark trousers, and heavy chaps left the bank and untied a pony at the rack. Mott Wingard mounted and rode down Houston Street. So he had beaten him out again, Jim realized. I could save myself five minutes right here, he thought.

He walked back to Moore's office, behind a moss-green cloth partition. He felt the curious eyes of the tellers turning to watch after he had passed. He rapped on the door, turned the knob, and went in. The partition rose only slightly above head height, and enclosed Moore's desk, a big Salamander safe, and some mahogany cabinets. The banker removed his spectacles to peer coldly at Jim.

"Don't tell me to knock," Jim said. "I just passed a test in that." He put his boot up on a chair.

"What's on your mind?" asked Moore.

"Money," said Jim.

"How much money?"

"Eighteen hundred. Payable in one week."

"What makes you think you can pay it?" Moore held up his spectacles to examine them for smudges.

Jim did not know how much he should say lest he involve Coe. "The money's in town. I'm buying Doctor

Neeley's cattle. When I deliver them I can collect and pay you back.''

"What did you have in mind for collateral?"

"My ranch."

Leaning back, the banker gave Jim a patronizing smile. "I don't know how much you know about banking procedure. But here's how a loan works—"

"Do I get the money?"

Moore bristled. "Who do you think you are, Canning? A man asking favors oughtn't to come in with a chip on his shoulder."

"You've got money to loan and I want to borrow some. Now, just say yes or no." Jim stood by the chair.

"No," said Ira Moore.

"All right. That makes everything plain. If I ever have any business again, you know the last place I'll take it. You know I'm in trouble, but you won't scratch your name on a check to help me, even with collateral you know is sound."

"That's what I don't know," Moore argued. "I can't risk bank money on a fly-by-night like you."

"My ranch isn't fly-by-night. It's been right there for quite a while. Henry Coe tells me Wingard's lease is invalid. So it's just a question of time until the property is negotiable."

"Mott Wingard tells me otherwise," said Moore.

Jim's hand swept the desk. The big ledger Moore had been working on crashed to the floor. Tall against the dull green drapes, he stood in the denim jacket whose sleeves were too short. A little blood had come through the bandage on his hand. His face was lean with hunger past satisfying.

"I wish I could have seen you with Wingard," he said. "Did you salute him? You didn't forget 'sir' did you? What did he buy you with—promises or threats?"

Moore stood up. Men were hurrying toward the enclosure. "You'd better get out of here!" warned Moore.

The door opened and a teller stood nervously in the opening. "Excuse me, Mr. Moore—we thought we heard something fall."

"You asked what I know about banking," Jim told Moore. "Not much. But I know quite a bit about men. I think I'll get vaccinated when I leave here. I feel like I'd been exposed to something I'd hate to catch."

There was a faint smell of fall in the air when he went out, a coolness, a blue bitterness of winter. He looked south and there they were—the big clouds that pushed up from Mexico, heavy and oxidized looking. He wished he were going to be in the hills when the rain came, sweeping like a broom, rustling the dry desert shrubs and battering the grasses down. But he would be here, horseless, ranchless, not quite friendless.

It was a fight in a dark room. Swing until you were exhausted without connecting. Then the floor smashed you as someone knocked you down. You began to wonder, *Why get up again?*

This town could help him. Maybe some of them wanted to help him. But they were afraid of Wingard, and of Adams, and perhaps of Jim himself. They were afraid even to be friends with a man running so close to trouble.

Wearily he began resorting his cards to see whether he could make a hand out of them still. Mario. Perhaps Mario would pay in advance after all. No, not if he had any sense. Doctor Neeley. *Excuse me, doctor, sir—I was wondering, sir, if you'd reconsider?*

He spat across the hitchrack. The habit of deference was slow to grow on a man. It was a craving many were born with and could not break; but if you didn't have it, it was hard to go to your banker or your merchant or your horse trader with your hat in your hand and conduct yourself like a lost dog.

A man gripped his arm. He turned his head, expecting

to see the marshal. Judge Coe was standing there, his expression resentful.

"Damn it, where've you been? I've hit every place you were likely to be and finally saw you from the window after I gave up."

"I didn't think you'd be down so early," Jim said. He watched a burro laden with firewood coming along the street. An old man was driving it with a switch.

"I get down before Shackelford's finished mixing acorn meal with the coffee. Have you seen anybody?"

"I made the deal with Mario."

"Good! How about Neeley?"

"I got his cows on consignment last night."

Coe hit him on the shoulder and began to smile.

"Saw Hawk this morning," Jim continued. "He's got a bullet hole in his left arm. I helped him change the bandage. He keeps a little string through the hole and when he pulls the string out it gets the matter draining. He let me throw the string in the street."

"The filthy—!"

"Oh, yeah—I talked to Horse Hammond about that buckskin. He's decided not to sell it to me."

"Why, he's had your name on that horse for months! What'd he say?" Coe was beginning to look less jubilant.

The mouse-colored, long-eared burro went by on its tiny hoofs while the old man trotted after it. "Oh, something about a bad hoof," Jim told the judge. "Then I got a note from Neeley saying he'd changed his mind. He'd have to have cash."

Coe muttered a prolonged curse.

"So I had a talk with Ira Moore. Wingard was just leaving as I went in. Moore gave me an imitation of a snake standing on its hind legs, but he's been crawling so long it wasn't very convincing. He doesn't make the rules, it seems like—he just—you know? Henry," he sighed, "this town's got an eye for a man in trouble that would make a buzzard start looking for some pencils and a tin cup. Folks around Frontera can hear a stomach growl three counties off."

Coe had a habit of clearing his throat when he was angry. He cleared it several times, and abruptly turned to enter the bank. Jim stepped back and caught his arm.

"I'll tell you how I feel about it, judge. If they don't want to shake loose because a man needs help, then they can keep it."

"Don't go proud on me now, Jim," said Coe sarcastically.

"I couldn't float two bits' worth of pride. This is something else. I picked up some mighty bad habits among all those thieves and badmen. The best we could, we took care of each other. It meant taking a hiding sometimes, or even giving your food to a man who needed it worse. The reason we did it was because it was us against them—the guards. If we hadn't all been fighting something, we'd have just been a bunch of men having the usual troubles, I suppose. That's what jolts me about people like this. Nobody's been asked to take a beating for me, or go out on a longer limb than you go out on right along. But they won't do it. They're scared. There's nobody in this town I give a damn for, now, except you and Mrs. Lee and Ann."

"Jim," said Coe, "when you're my age you'll realize three people you can count on is a pretty fair showing for one town. People don't want to be cowards—most of them just are, when the pinch comes. So we've got a Christian duty to jar them out of it, haven't we? That's why I'm going into the bank, now, and you're going to wait right here."

"What I'm trying to say is that if I make it at all, I'll make it alone. Just so I can square with Moore and the rest."

"What I'm going to do won't spoil that ambition a-tall," Coe said. "I'm just going to terminate all my business with the bank. I'll find loans for my clients in Marfa. I'll keep my own money in my safe. You see, I just don't feel right, aiding and abetting a fellow like Moore."

Chapter 15

WHILE JIM WAITED he heard Marshal Adams's voice around the corner. "Here now, Hosay! What's a-hurry?"

He moved to the corner. Up Clay Street the marshal had stopped the old man with the burro. The firewood, an enormous load of roots and small branches, had the appearance of a haystack with small, dainty legs and hoofs keeping it just off the ground. The woodcutter removed his hat and held it against his stomach.

"Sí Señor Gavilán?"

Leaning against a tie-rail, tall, supple and offensively self-confident, Marshal Adams made a gesture with the little rum-soaked cigar he was lighting. "Unload."

The old man's arm slowly descended with the switch. "Here, *Señor Gavilán?"*

"Right where you stand, old man. I'm kinda curious to see how many bottles you're freightin' under all them twigs."

"But, señor—all day yesterday—"

Adams finished lighting the cigar and slung the match at him. "Now, dad blister your behind, Hosay, I said *unload!"*

In a moment the woodcutter had dropped the load to the ground. The twisted, thorny branches were made up in small bunches. But it had probably taken an hour to load the burro, Jim knew. There was no tequila in the load.

Jim returned to the front of the bank to wait as the Mexican began reloading. In a few moments Adams sauntered around the corner. Adams passed with a sober glance. Crossing the street, he made his way toward the Big Corner Saloon. Jim watched him, hating the slow swagger of the slim hips and the bright bulk of the gun he wore on his thigh. A man lurched from a foot alley and came unsteadily down the walk. All at once he saw the marshal. He pulled his hat down and leaned quickly against a store front in an effort to appear sober and anonymous. Adams stopped and gravely inspected him.

"Howdy, John," he said. "Where you been keepin' yourself?"

The face of the drunk came up. "Why, hello, marshal. Got a job, now, and workin' steady."

"You got another one now, John, seeing as you're drinkin' so steady."

"Why, marshal, that ain't so."

"Stand up," snapped Adams. "Let's see how you look away from that wall."

The drunk straightened, weaving delicately in the manner of a table knife balanced on one's finger. Adams thrust his boot between the man's feet and gave a quick twist. The drunk staggered and sat down.

"You better hike up to the jail and wait for me," Adams said. "I got some cordwood that wants choppin'. Finest conditioner in the world for you one-beer fellers." He walked on.

Coe came from the bank and handed Jim a bank draft and some gold pieces. Jim looked at them in surprise.

"He made me take it," said Coe. "The check's for the cattle; the cash is for a horse and anything else you need. You see, I can hurt Ira worse than Wingard can. So he trades with me. But you'd better shove, Jim, before somebody comes along that can hurt him worse than I can."

"Judge," said Jim, "if I ever said we weren't *amigos*—"

"Take off," said Coe.

At dusk a moist wind brought the clouds up from across

the river. Mott Wingard came from a restaurant with Tom Elrod. Ed was supposed to have been there, but he had not shown up and they had eaten without him. He was probably having some drinks at the Big Corner, Wingard concluded, and he walked in that direction.

"Gonna be a wet one," said Elrod, looking up at the clouds above the roof lines of Houston Street.

Wingard paced along glumly. He hated inactivity; all day he had been drinking coffee and whisky, until his stomach was tender and his nerves were raw. But he had put a lid on Canning and he needed to keep an eye on things.

They went into the saloon and heard a clatter of pool balls. Halfway down the room the pool tables were grouped under a brass chandelier with four pipelike arms supporting carbide lamps. The saloon smelled of fresh sawdust. Pierce, the saloonkeeper, had seen wet weather coming. There were green-topped game tables at the right of the door. At the left was the bar. Behind it was a mirror nearly as long as the bar and ornately set in a walnut frame which looked like part of a bedroom suite.

"Ed around?" Wingard growled at Pierce.

Pierce was a slightly paunchy man with a fleshy face. His dark hair was thin and always neatly brushed. He spent more time among the game tables than behind the bar, and through some sense of fitness only poured drinks for important customers. He reached for Wingard's special bottle and set out two glasses.

"Ain't seen Ed all day," yawned Pierce. "Seen Adams. Seen Ira Moore. Seen lots of other people."

"Seen our good friend Canning?" asked Tom Elrod.

"Him neither. Here comes a friend of yours, though."

Wingard saw Marshal Adams come in and gravely sweep the room with a glance. He knew Adams had seen him, but the marshal gave no indication. Adams sauntered to the card tables, and stopped behind a tall, thin gambler who ran the games for Pierce. The gambler pushed out some chips and said, "Up two bucks."

The other players peeked at their cards again and the dealer waited. Hawk Adams drawled, "It's your funeral, Crane. But you've got more nerve than I have, to bet on that hand."

He drifted on.

Pierce swore. "Scratch one gambler!" he said. "Crane took him for fifteen bucks one night and he's been doing that to him ever since. I'm going to miss him," he sighed.

A man slowed before the saloon. Wingard made out a dark, hatless head above the frosted glass portion of the window. He watched him move close to the glass and peer into the saloon. It was Felipe Vasquez. His eyes touched Wingard's, he raised one finger briefly, and left.

Wingard gazed at Elrod. "Take your time, Tom. I'm going to check the restaurant again. Maybe Ed's developed an appetite by now."

Felipillo was back on his high stool behind the counter when the cattleman entered. Wingard's nose wrinkled at the odors of dust and lime. A few candles burned in the necks of bottles on the tables and a single lamp hung from the ceiling. The cantina held the dank coolness of a cellar. A drunk was asleep at one table with his head on his arm. Three other men were arguing over cards.

Felipillo plucked a string and made it thrum, played a final chord, smiled at Wingard, and laid the guitar on the bar. He was trying to grow a mustache; thin, silken hairs darkened his lip. He set out a glass, wiped a flyspeck from the rim with his fingertip, and poured mescal, Wingard's Mexican drink.

"I don't know whether this would interest you," he said.

"My interests get wider all the time," said Wingard. Earlier that day Felipillo had informed him of the meeting of Jim Canning and Ámador.

"Canning found a horse somewhere," said Felipillo.

"That horse-trader, Hammond!" Wingard exclaimed.

"No—it wasn't Luskey's buckskin. A chestnut. He left about two hours ago."

"Two hours! Why didn't you tell me when he left?"

"I couldn't find you. And Ámador left this morning."

Wingard let the mescal cauterize his throat. "Well, they won't be hard to find. Have you seen Ed?"

"No, sir. But I can find him. I'll get a boy to mind the shop."

"When you find him, tell him I'm waiting at the feed barn."

He drained the small glass, dug a nickel-sized gold piece from the tight trousers, and dropped it in the sound box of the guitar like a coin into a blind man's cup. "Buy yourself a cheap cigar," he suggested.

Felipillo sighed, began to shake the coin from the instrument, and said in valiant good humor, "Everybody does that!"

"You shouldn't be working for so many people," Wingard told him. He returned to the saloon to pick up Elrod. Out in the chilly evening, he said, "We're going out to the camp again. Canning's left."

It was a half hour before Ed appeared at the feed barn. "Where the devil have you been?" asked his father.

"I stopped to give Neeley hell about last night."

Ed wore an expression of truculence. He had not shaved and his jaws and chin were rough with golden stubble. Something about his face caused Wingard to look away. In a moment he would be coming to some unfortunate conclusions about his son. "Come on," he growled, heading for the harness room.

"*Now* where we going?"

"Get your saddle," snapped his father.

While they saddled, Horse Hammond kept out of sight. Silverware clattered in the room where he lived. They rode from the barn. Turning left, Mott Wingard began buttoning the metal snaps of his long coat. The stock of a rifle protruded from under his knee.

"Canning's bought those cows of Neeley's," he said. "Neeley have anything to say about it?"

"He told me Canning dug up the cash," Ed said.

"Either he's lying or Moore is. Somebody's lying, and I'm going to know who."

"Somebody out here in the cactus going to tell you who?" Ed challenged.

"Somebody out here in the cactus is planning to move some cattle to Mexico. I'm planning to stop him."

From his coat pocket, Ed slipped a half-pint bottle and pulled the cork with his teeth. Wingard reached over and slapped it down. Both horses shied.

"What the hell was that for?" demanded Ed.

"That was for keeping your head clear while I talk. It's bad manners to get stoned while a man's talking to you, Ed."

The silence was brittle. Ed stared fiercely at his father. The chilly, rain-smelling wind blew against their faces and hissed through the head-high mesquite alongside the road.

Elrod said heartily, "Stopping them cows will be no trouble. Little outfit of cows like that; and more'n likely only Canning and the Mexican pushin' 'em."

"But hell won't have us," Wingard told them, "if we wind up in the marshal's office again."

"We called his bluff before, didn't we?" Ed contended.

" 'We' were lucky," said Wingard sarcastically. " 'We' stopped him with a jolt to the jaw. Then it turned out Canning was willing to trade with us. He didn't press charges against you for carving his hand in exchange for my not charging him with assault against me. Otherwise he'd be on his way back to Huntsville and you'd be waiting to stand trial. Never count too heavy on us doing it again. Adams is a queer bird. There's no predicting him. I thought at first it was just jailbirds he liked to kick around. Now I've about decided it's a matter of his needing a face to step on and he doesn't care whose."

"That gives me a great idea," said Ed. "Let's go back to town and let Adams step on Canning's face instead of ours."

Wingard closed his eyes. When my time comes, he thought, I'll sell everything and sink it in a trust fund. Otherwise, in one week, Ed will spend it all on stick candy, monkeys on strings, and girls in sequined underwear. God in heaven, he thought bitterly, he no more understands ranching or range politics than he understands how to knit socks. What smoothed the edges of his temper a bit was a recollection of Ed's tirade the other night—he was still mortgaged to that infantile hand Canning had given him.

"The point is this," said the rancher. "Canning will try to break my lease, now that Coe's advising him. It won't stand even a low-power inspection because he signed it in prison without a proper witness. So I'd rather the subject didn't come up, officially. It won't if he stays broke. He'll stay broke if his career as a commission man ends before it starts. If Neeley backed down and let him have the cows, then he'll be the saddest sawbones in Texas when Canning drags his chin back to town with nothing but sunburn and sad news. If Canning raised the cash, then *he's* the big loser. Either way Canning's still broke. And not about to have any consignment cows forced on him. Now do you savvy?" he asked.

"Uh-huh," Ed said, like a man who had sat through a lecture on something he already understood. He smiled. "Maybe we'll bag an antelope or something to make it worthwhile."

A coldness like gray iron touched Wingard. For a moment he thought of sending Ed back. "Understand me, Ed! You had your circus last time. This is a cow chase, not a man hunt. Anything that drops better have four legs. Clear?"

Ed inserted a black Mexican cigarette between his lips. He struck a small block of wax matches to get a light. The sulphurous explosion left the men half blinded.

"Sure. Clear as a bell!" he said. "Damn, it's starting to rain."

Chapter 16

IN THE NIGHT the rain increased, pelting cold and dark on the corrugated iron roof of Neeley's line shack. Jim heard it splattering on the ground. He had met Amador here at dusk. The wind tested the cracks between the mud plaster and mesquite branches, and it was good to be in dry blankets. In the morning it was still raining. They made coffee and ate hardtack and jerky. They pulled on slickers before going out to saddle.

The cattle were not hard to gather. For some time Neeley had been having hay hauled out and dumped at several spots, and although there was fair graze everywhere, the feed-lot cattle patronized the wispy, trampled remnants of the last loads of hay, raising their muzzles to bellow at the sky. The men got them moving down the creek. The rain made their horns glisten, their wet hides steam. About noon the rain ceased, and a short time later the clouds pulled apart to show a sky of the blue and silver of an Indian necklace.

The wash made it easy to drive the steers. They moved down through the hills toward the desert. As they neared Jim's home place, he rode ahead to scout it. From the hill, he looked down upon it. It looked quiet in the afternoon sunshine, the leaves of the trees sparkling after the rain, the ground dark. He could hear jays fussing in the big cottonwood tree. Supporting the barrel of Henry Coe's rifle, his bandaged hand pointed at the trampled place in the yard where they had thrown him like a horse that day.

And he felt again the tearing pain of the knife passing through his hand. It began to throb again with the painful memory.

After a few minutes he rode back to the herd.

"Did Coe tell you about my friendship with the Wingards?" he asked Mario.

The Mexican shrugged. "Maybe we get there, maybe we don't. It's war, eh?"

Jim smiled. "With an attitude like that, you'll never be surprised."

They passed the ranch buildings. Beyond, the hills were steep and rocky. Meadows opened out along the creek. Everything was fresh and damp, and Jim began to feel good about it. He could look at the creek and the hills and think, I'm coming back here. Not tomorrow; but when I come it will be with a court order. In the meantime he was on the best medicine in the world—work, the Sloan's liniment of the spirit.

That night, having put most of the high country behind them, they bedded the herd in a stretch of grass and rocks west of the river. Wingard used to call this his hospital: it had the rich graze of the mountains, the warm desert sun and wind. Not far below, the creek split into two small streams which wound down the rimrock toward the Rio Grande.

They staked the horses and made a fire upstream from the herd. The narrowness of the canyon would keep them from straying downstream. Jim sat with a cup of black coffee steaming in his hands, remembering things he had almost forgotten.

"I used to hunt arrowheads here," he told Mario. "Once in a while in the old days the Comanches would stop here to barbecue a *hacendado* after they'd been raiding in Mexico."

"For some *hacendados*," remarked Mario, "the best possible end."

Jim glanced at a cliff below the meadow. "That was their lookout. I found a cooking pot up there with the remains of a meal in it. It seems like fifty years ago, now."

As they gazed at the bluff, a spark of light gleamed on the rim of it and fell a short distance before it died out.

"Maybe they're cooking up there now," said Mario.

Jim reached for the carbine at his feet. He was touched by sudden apprehension. As he scrutinized the cliff, he slipped the gun off safety. It was too far for anything smaller than a man standing near the rim to be visible.

"I think that was a cigarette," he said. "I think there's somebody up there. Get your horse."

He girthed up quickly and rode back to meet the Mexican at the fire. They peered up the stair-stepping wall of rock.

"A man could do nothing from there," said Mario.

"He could start a rock-slide."

"But the cattle are upstream from the rocks."

"He could start it in the morning when we drive them through."

"How does a man get up there?"

"From here," Jim speculated, "he'd have to cross the creek and climb on foot. Or else ride back a half mile and take a trail up a canyon. That would take an hour. And we couldn't leave the cattle. Maybe that's why they threw the cigarette—to draw us away from the cattle."

But a man who wanted to be seen would not make so small a display as that, he realized. Unless someone down here was watching for it.

"We'll have to scout up-canyon," he decided. "If we don't see anything, you can come back and I'll try to get up there. But it'll be dark soon."

They rode toward the creek. It was damp and still. Jim heard a fish jump in a quiet pool. He glanced up at the bluff again, and just then his pony quivered and he curbed it sharply. Now he heard horses running, and he and Mario looked at each other. The sounds were coming closer but echoes made them hard to locate. Then the horses clattered around a turn above them and came run-

ning downstream behind a screen of willows, across the
creek. Jim swung quickly toward the camp, where there
was the shelter of boulders if this became a shooting fight.
Mario came with him.

They pulled in to watch two riders break from cover a
hundred yards below and cross the creek toward the herd.
In the dusk the cattle could be heard starting to move. Now
Jim saw what was going to happen, and that it was all
going to take place downstream. He looked up at the cliff
to see how that part of it was going. The men up there were
doing well. A rock which appeared tiny was descending in
long, smooth plunges, striking a ledge and bounding off to
smash into others farther down. Another large rock de-
tached itself from the cap rock. This time he saw a man
standing with a long pole or pry bar. Jim put the rifle to his
shoulder and aimed high. The gun jolted him and the horse
began to pitch. He curbed it, losing his hat as it bucked,
and the shot roared and echoed in the canyon. Mario
pulled up beside him.

"*Qué pues? Qué pasa?*"

The first of the boulders thundered against the detritus
at the base of the bluff. Fragments of stone ripped the
willows. Through the echoes of falling rocks could be
heard a high, whooping clamor as the riders stampeded
the cattle. The herd began streaming down the meadow.

"Let's try to turn them!" Jim shouted. The cattle were
coming from the far rim of the meadow where they had
been bunched. There was still time to cross in front of
them and work them away from the bluff before they ran
into the rock slide. Jim smacked the pony with the stock of
the gun. He heard the Mexican following him. In the
smoky dusk he saw glints of clacking horns and heard the
desperate bellowing of the herd.

He made the far side of the meadow and swerved to pry
the cattle from the base of the hill into the creek. Then he
saw Mario. He had fallen with his horse in the path of the
herd. He was standing there hatless, trying to mount the
frightened pony. Jim started to ride back; but it was plain

that he could not reach him. He rode along the edge of the herd, firing at the leaders. When he glanced at the Mexican again, he saw him mounted and holding the horse while the cattle broke around them like a mud-flow.

Jim rode with the cattle, shouting, and crowding the nearest ones. A few broke behind him and went on down the canyon, where the gray rock dust boiled like smoke. He turned the others and they crashed into the willows and brush. Water flew to spray as they hit the creek. Then it was a confusion of running steers and falling steers and the noise of their bawling. He went through the water and stopped on a sand bar to look back.

Mario was pushing some of the stragglers along toward the creek. Jim sat there breathing hard. Something ripped the willows near him and an instant later a gunshot crashed at his left and not far away. He saw the flash among the rocks, and fired back before he had made out his target. A man spurred from the shadows, fired twice at him and then swerved his horse to gallop west toward the long slope at the back of the meadow. The light struck him now as Jim took aim, and he saw and knew Ed Wingard's horse, saw and knew his black Stetson and the slim look of him in the saddle. Slowly he lowered the rifle. No, he thought, let him be the one that tried to get me—not me the one that got him. Now we've got something to chew over with Marshal Adams.

He pushed the cattle a little farther and turned back, hunting for the Mexican. He saw him crossing the meadow as if he were searching for Jim, but he was riding south. Then Jim saw him wave his rifle and pick his pony up into an easy lope, riding now toward a rider near the slope. Jim saw that it was Ed Wingard, waiting there while the Mexican came closer. Jim shouted, but the Mexican could not hear him. Wingard raised the rifle coolly. Then Mario knew it was not Jim, and he brought his Colt up swiftly and fired a long, hopeless shot across the grass. It missed, and Ed's shot came heavy and sure. Mario fell back, groped for the saddle horn, and fell from the saddle. Jim spurred across the shallow stream as Ed turned and loped up the hill.

Night was settling in. In the dusk he found Mario and looked down at him. He lay face down, his arms reaching. Jim knelt beside him. Turning him over, he pulled his shirt open, but immediately closed it again on the large wound below his collar bone. Mario was not breathing. Far up the slope he heard the horses struggling in the loose shale of the rock slide.

After a time it was quiet except for the bawling of cattle. The meadow was dark, cool, and moist. Occasionally a loose rock would come sprawling down the bluff and land with a clean, splintering crash. Jim moved the Mexican's body back to camp and dug a grave with a hand ax. He wrapped him in a tarpaulin, took everything from his pockets, and after burying him piled stones on the grave. He made a roll of things which had belonged to him. Someone in Chihuahua would want them.

Then he rode out to look for the horse. Now and then he heard it moving along the base of the hill. Close to where Ed had waited for Mario to come in range, he found a hat. He picked it up. It was Ed's black Stetson, with that silver cord. Jim put his finger through a bullet hole in the crown. He looked inside it and saw a small fold of leather tucked under the sweatband. It was only a couple of inches square, and inside was a smudged picture of Ann Neeley.

He rode back and lay among the rocks to wait.

Things were different now. They sent men to the penitentiary for a little thing like cutting someone's hand. So what would they do about this? They would, he hoped, put a rope around Ed's neck and hang him. He would let Adams handle all the arrangements. No doubt he was very efficient when he really had something to work on.

A stone clattered across the meadow. They had left the horses somewhere above and were walking. Jim made out three shapes searching among the boulders of the meadow. He squirmed around into position, took long and patient aim, and squeezed the trigger. Bright and huge, the shot blasted the roof off the night. Briefly he saw the men, then heard them shouting. He fired repeatedly and the echoes crashed and tumbled like stones. The heavy carbine went empty.

Shots came back at him, hitting high and low and wide. The men were blinded by their own gun flashes. He rose and ran back to where his horse was trying to break loose from the picket-pin. He had tied everything he needed behind the cantle. He was on the creek trail before they stopped firing into the rocks.

Chapter 17

THERE WAS NOT one blasted thing they could do, Mott Wingard realized, except to roost all night on the hillside above the meadow and wait for light. And he waited with cold and savage patience. For if Ed's Stetson were still down there, the wait was a good investment. If Canning had found it and taken off, then there was hell and hair-pulling ahead. But if he were still there it would be the best break possible. They would extinguish Canning like a cigarette.

Wingard looked on it as an act of war, not as a killing. Canning had made war when he knocked him out of the saddle the other day. If he were still forted up there, it would not take long to do what had to be done, to bury him so deep in some lost canyon that the buzzards and coyotes would pass over the spot without knowing it. And Canning's career as a field general would be over.

Wingard knew now that he was fighting for more than a piece of land. He was fighting for the right to tell a man, *Do this, Do that,* and know it would be done. To make or break a merchant, to swing a county election involving public lands he wanted to buy, to get roads built—all the things they meant when they said, *Takes money to make money.* To look at himself in the mirror when he shaved and know he was not over the hill by a damned sight—that he was going to be a lot bigger still before he finished.

When he had annexed Three Deuces, he would know and everyone would know that he was still calling the shots for Socorro County.

Gray and thin, dawn seeped over the hills into the meadow. The men saw nothing there but some cattle, a rifle, and a mound of rocks near a fuming fire ring.

"Well, that's that," Wingard growled wearily. He gave Ed the elbow to rouse him. "Wake up. We're riding."

"Where to?" yawned Ed. He had slept hard with his head on his arms, and his face was creased.

"Tom and I are going to town. You're going to camp at Deuces until I send for you."

Ed was swallowing the taste in his mouth.

"Like hell! I'm going to Pierce's and have six drinks without stopping." He turned to climb the hill.

Wingard seized him by the front of his shirt. "Don't be telling me how it's going to be, boy! Not *this* morning! You'll stay at the ranch. And if anybody but me or Tom comes, you'd better be ready to ride, cowboy. Because it'll mean you've finally dumped over a pail of slops even your old man can't mop up!"

Ed scoffed. "I can handle Adams. Him and anybody else he brings along. Let them try and take me."

"Oh, you can handle him all right! You can handle anything. In a pig's eye! You're going to sit right there with a gun on the table and your eyes on the trail, and write one thousand times, *I will keep my gun in the holster after this.*"

Ed wiped his mouth and stared at his father with smoky resentment. Near by, Tom Elrod was frowning up the hill at the horses, cross-tied among some cedars.

"I've got to find out how the wind blows before you show your face around Frontera," Wingard said finally. "If I think we've got a chance, I'll get a lawyer down from El Paso. If it looks bad, you'll have to take off for Chihuahua. You can stay there as long as you need to. Dollars will buy a man a pretty fair life in Chihuahua City."

"If you like your food greasy and your girls dark," Ed

scoffed. "You fixed it before with Canning. You can fix it again." Then he said, with a warped grin of inspiration, "I'm not so sure *I* hit him anyway! I heard Tom blastin' away up there!"

Elrod regarded him with calm contempt. "Sure," he said, "I shot him, and all you did was lose a hat. Maybe you can be the first man in Texas to get hung for losing a hat."

Wingard grabbed Ed by the neck. His thick, strong fingers closed like a trap. Ed choked and struggled, while the rancher panted, "Is this the way you want it—*like this?* Only with a rope? We're not arguing about a poker hand—we're talking about somebody getting the box kicked out from under his feet!"

He opened his hands and let Ed stumble away. "Now, wake up!" he growled. "Make up your mind to stay out of sight and keep a horse saddled."

Ed started up the hill, tall and loose-limbed. A sudden pity flooded Mott Wingard as he looked at him. In one instant he was seeing twenty-two years of the boy, breathing the smoke of all the memories and ambitions that had revolved around Ed, which now he sadly realized were bad debts on which he would never collect. Now at last he could not blame himself for all of Ed's failings, because they had been there a long time. He had been viewing his son with the foolish affection of a father. And this was the saddest truth of all: Ed would never be any more of a man than he was right now.

Jim reached Frontera at nine-fifteen that morning. He was so tired he had a feeling of floating. Halting before the hotel, he was aware of not having shaved in two days, of being crusted with dirt and mud, and he knew how choice he looked to the men sitting on the gallery of the hotel. They watched him dismount, snap a tie rope about the horse's neck, and tie him solid to the hitching rail. With one hand he loosened the cinches, then took the soiled canvas roll and the black Stetson from behind the saddle.

Carrying them under his arm, he looked up and down the street. The green shades of the bank were raised, a little spring wagon was being loaded with provisions across the road, and women in long summer dresses were shopping.

Looking at all this traffic of a busy cattle town, Jim thought: They probably think they have problems. The children aren't sleeping well; they can't make ends meet; father shouldn't stop at the saloon on the way home. Well, he could tell them these weren't problems, just episodes. A problem was when a man fell in a well and there was no one within fifty miles who wasn't afraid of falling in if he tried to help you out.

It was a hot, humid morning. But the stair well to Coe's office was dark and cool. There was a note on the door. *At Court.* That's right, the man worked, didn't he? Hard to remember everything hadn't stopped because a circus had come to town. Jim sat in Coe's deep chair with his head tipped back against the leather and his long legs extended. His body thrummed with exhaustion. His hand pulsed with pain.

He thought about the Wingards. Had they stayed out there to look for Ed's Stetson? Or had Elrod waited and the Wingards come in? That hat was pretty damned important now.

Jim sat up with a grunt and buried his face in his hands. He had hidden the saddle gun in the mesquite outside of town. He was almost afraid to leave the office without it. At last he descended to the hot, bright street and saw two boys looking at his horse; he realized the word had already been passed.

"You boys want to make a quarter?" he asked them. "Tell Judge Coe I'm in town. I'll be in his office or at the jail."

"Yes, sir," a boy with two long front teeth gasped.

Carrying the hat and the canvas roll, Jim walked slowly up Clay Street through the brilliant light and shadow of the trees. He rapped on the frame of the flimsy mosquito-netted door.

"Yeah?" Adams's voice came like the growl of a bear. But seeing Jim he brightened. "Missed you yesterday," he said amiably:

He was tipped back in his chair with his thumbs under his cartridge belt, a big, oily-skinned man in dark pants and a white shirt discolored under the arms by perspiration. Intent and pock-marked, he watched Jim lay the stained roll of canvas on his desk. Jim punched out the crown of the Stetson the way Ed wore it. He moved the slide up the silver cord. He looked at Adams.

"I had you on my list," he said. "But something happened to keep me from getting back to town. I got bushwhacked."

Adams leaned forward. Resting one elbow on the roll, he gazed solemnly at Jim. "You don't mean it! And you never done a thing to start it?"

"I was driving some cattle down Cuero Canyon. Do you remember the man I was with at the cantina?"

"Told you you were in bad company," reminded the marshal.

"I won't be in it again. He's dead."

Adams sat back quickly. He frowned, then the skin of his brow smoothed and a glint of pleasure kindled in his face. "Why, sho'!" he said. "How'd this terrible thing happen?"

Jim told the story, while Adams's hands carefully peeled the canvas from the collection of Mario's belongings. They seemed somehow dismally feeble proof that such a man had ever lived. A gold watch, a large brass key, some small cigars, a match safe, and a set of folding steel eating utensils.

"This all his stuff?" asked Adams.

"All but his camp gear. I buried him in the canyon."

Adams wagged his head. "Dead, eh? Ain't that astonishing!" He swung the watch by the chain. "Right fancy timepiece for a goatherder, eh?"

Jim did not comment. Adams shot a look at him. "You say it was two Wingards and one Elrod?"

"That's all I saw, just the three of them."

"Will you take a Bible oath that you saw 'em?"

"I saw one man on the bluff," Jim repeated. "I saw two horse-backers cross the creek and stampede the cattle."

"How do you know it was Ed that shot the Mexican?"

"Because he was pot shooting at me first. He was close enough that he should have had me, but he must have been nervous. I scared him off with a couple of close ones and he rode away. Then I saw him laying for Mario. He took his time over the shot, and the Mexican got a bullet through his hat before Ed killed him."

Jim turned the hat to put his finger through the bullet hole in the brim. "This is Ed's Stetson, and there's the bullet hole. Ámador's out there and there's a bullet hole in him. I claim that's a pretty fair case."

"Shall I write that up?"

"Write whatever it takes to swear out a warrant."

Adams pushed the articles aside, found paper and a pen in the desk, and began writing. "Details, details!" he sighed, with the deepest pleasure in his voice. *"Sworn before me this*—what the hell's the date?—*eighth day of September—Township of Frontera, County of Socorro—grand and glorious State of T-e-x-a-s. U.S.A.,"* he added. *"Comes now James Canning, who deposeth and says—"*

Jim read it and signed his name. The bandage on his left hand steadied the paper. Adams smiled as he reread the affidavit. "Seen any of them since?" he inquired.

"No, I came on in. I figure they may have stayed to hunt that Stetson."

Adams tried it on, found it small, grinned, and hung it on a wall hook. He was humming. "Can't blame 'em for that. It's probably the most expensive hat John B. Stetson ever turned out. Where will you be at if I want you?"

"At the doctor's for a while. Then I'll be somewhere or other. You know, I'd feel safer if I had a gun."

"I expect you would," Adams agreed. "Hey, that

bandage is beginning to smell. I'll bet you wind up with a meat hook just about like Ed's.''

The boys Jim had sent to the courthouse were waiting in the street, squatting against the wall. As he came out, they rose, excited. Years from now, he supposed, they'll remember how a man with cold gray eyes sent them on an errand, and later—later, what? Maybe they would remember how a man named Wingard hunted all over town looking for the man to keep him from saying things in court about his son. And how the fugitive had no gun to defend himself with, so— So what *did* a man in a corner defend himself with?

''Judge Coe ain't there, Mister Canning,'' said the boy with the teeth like a squirrel. ''He's out to Toler's ranch making out a will.''

''You boys busy?'' Jim smiled.

''No, sir.''

''Will you wait right here then? And if the judge comes tell him I'm at Doctor Neeley's. I'll come back when I get through.''

''Yes, sir!'' The lad caught the coin Jim tossed.

Chapter 18

ON THE HOTEL gallery Henry Coe and some other men were keeping books on the street traffic when Jim returned. Coe was sitting two chairs from the nearest man and was talking with no one. He rose and came down the steps, tight-lipped and red. Taking Jim's arm, he guided him to the corner.

"Adams is waiting for you," he said tersely. "Something new. He wouldn't say what. I've picked up scraps of stories about you. Why the devil didn't you write it down and leave it on my desk? Damn it, am I your lawyer or not?"

"Just absent-minded," Jim sighed. "Well, Mario was right. I told him it might be risky and he said, 'It's war.' He died in that war."

Coe listened. "Then, by God," he exclaimed, "Wingard's finished!"

"All he'll have left is money," Jim said wryly. "But the strange thing is that there's hardly a man in Huntsville with more money than he can carry in a Bull Durham sack."

"All right, but there's a few. And to keep on having his kind of money you need prestige. The power to put your friends in places where they can help you. You can't do that if your son was hanged for murder and a half-wit blind man could see you were with him on the ride. So they murdered Mario," he said gloomily. "It's a letter I'm going to hate to write to his parents. But a case I'll enjoy

131

hearing.''

It was noon, now, and growing hotter, and as they entered the marshal's office Jim saw Hawk Adams fanning himself with a palm-leaf fan. In a corner sat a slim, sober young Mexican with the neckband of his shirt buttoned but wearing no necktie. His nose was long, his eyes pale, and the mustache on his lip was no thriftier than it had looked the last time Jim saw him in his father's cantina. Felipe Vasquez glanced down as Jim began to smile at him. Adams was pouring himself a drink of water from a terra-cotta jug slung in a window.

''It's a small world, boys,'' he told the men heartily. ''This young fella came to report a stolen hat. One of his good customers was shacked up in his back room last night sleepin' off a big one. This morning his hat was gone. Ain't that mysterious?''

Coe began a harsh chuckling. Jim smiled at the Mexican as he sat stiffly gazing out the window, his face flushed. Turning impulsively, Felipillo spoke to the marshal.

''It's true, *Señor Gavilán!* He was drunk, you know, and left the hat on the table. And somebody took it. It was Mr. Ed Wingard—I guess you know him.''

''Oh, I think we've met socially once or twice,'' said Adams soberly. ''Tall sort of chap? Fires his gun around kind of loose-like?''

Felipillo shrugged and looked away.

''Why didn't Mr. Ed Wingard report this serious loss himself?'' asked the marshal.

''He was feeling *crudo*, you know, so he's gone out to the ranch to work it off. He asked me to tell you about it.''

''How long ago did his father get in town?'' Jim asked him.

''I have not seen his father,'' said Felipillo stiffly.

The marshal placed himself before him, one hand on his hip, holding his cup of water by the handle. ''You know what I bet?'' he said. ''I bet somebody else's been dropping money in your git-tar. That's the damndest lie I ever did hear!''

"No, sir! It's the truth, *Señor Gavilán!* He was there most of yesterday and all last—"

Adams began pouring the water over the Mexican's slicked down hair. "You damn little grease ant," he chuckled as Felipillo scrambled from the chair. "I thought you were one chili-picker a man could count on. Sit down," he said. *"Sit down!"* he bellowed when Felipillo hesitated. Felipillo dropped on the chair.

"Now. How much did Wingard give you to say that?"

"I promise it's the truth!" gasped Felipillo. "I swear—"

"Canning, get that Bible out of my desk," said Adams. "I use it to press flowers in, but I reckon it'll handle an oath as well as another one. No, wait a minute. This feller probably don't use a Protestant Bible. You a Catholic, Phil?"

"Sí, señor." Water was trickling from Felipillo's heavy hair down over his face.

Adams's big forefinger hooked the thin gold chain from the man's shirt collar. A small crucifix hung from it.

"Take holt here, boy. If you're gonna swear, you better swear by something you believe in. No crossed fingers in this office. Now just tell me again about Ed drinkin' at your place."

A fear deeper than fear of the marshal clouded the tan face. "You know, *Señor Gavilán,* maybe I ought to talk to a lawyer. I don't know about these—these law matters."

"What the Nelly you want with a lawyer, junior? You're just makin' a sworn statement before me and this retired knife-thrower and the judge. Talk to him if you want a lawyer. Come on! Else I'll know you've been lyin' to me, and it's a fact I can't rightly say what'll happen to you next."

Jim could hear Felipillo breathing as though he had been running. Sitting there with his shirt and face wet, he seemed to shrink from the crucifix hanging against his chest. Suddenly the marshal smacked the back of his hand against Felipillo's cheek. Felipillo rocked on the chair. Jim could still hear the loud breathing, and he realized then that it was Hawk Adams he heard. Adams smashed the pottery cup on the floor, clenched both fists, and loomed above the Mexican like a tree. Blood surged into his face.

"You gonna swear?" he shouted. Felipillo cringed against the wall. Adams hit him again. *"You gonna swear?* You louse-crawlin' little nance, did you figger I was simple-minded or something? Little Ed's in the soup this time, and no greasy fingers the size of yours are going to fish him out! He's Hawk's this time, savvy? *He's Hawk's!"*

He wheeled to his desk, picked up a paper, and shoved it into the Mexican's face. "There's your statement! Tear it up. Else grab holt of that tin cross you're freightin' and nail it down where God can see it."

The screen door creaked open and Jim turned just as a big, swarthy man with a straw sombrero on the back of his head stepped into the room. Adams turned swiftly. Mott Wingard stared at him but did not acknowledge Felipe Vasquez even by a glance. Wingard's eyes were bloodshot; but he was freshly shaven and smelled of witch hazel. His mustache had been trimmed. But the wrinkles of bone weariness were buried so deeply in his face that no barber could tease them out. About him there was a cinder-like hardness of fatigue.

"What's all the uproar?" he asked. "I could hear it half a block away."

Hawk Adams appeared pleased. "Oh, just a dry old legal matter, Mister Wingard," he said. "Felipillo, here, was about to depose and say something."

Wingard's mouth turned in a smile that was a grimace. "It sounded more like somebody was being asked to cease and desist!"

"What can we do for you?" asked Adams politely. He rubbed his long, strong hands together.

Wingard's brow creased. "I came to make a complaint.

My foreman was checking over on Cuero yesterday and found signs of a bunch of cattle being driven over my land.''

"Got your man right here!'' said Adams. "Jim Canning's already confessed to that crime.''

Jim looked at the rancher and waited for him to take it up. No one said a word, and Wingard could be seen trying to decide how far matters had progressed—whether to attack or retreat.

"I knew who it was, of course,'' Wingard said, staring at Jim.

"Then why come to the marshal?'' asked Jim. "Can't you handle a jailbird and a Mexican rebel?''

"I can. But that's Adams's job.''

"It was your job last night,'' Jim said. He felt his mouth drying.

"Does somebody want to post me on what's going on here?'' demanded the rancher.

Jim said, "Yes, I'll post you,'' and caught Wingard unprepared as he swung. His fist cracked against the rancher's cheekbone. Wingard sprawled against the door and fell halfway outside. Jim reached down, seized his boots, and hauled him back into the room. He dropped astraddle the rancher who was swinging wildly at his head. He blocked Wingard's blows with his forearms. Wingard's fists struck with massive power. Jim drove a chopping punch to his face. Adams and the judge had him by the arms then, and dragged him off; he kicked at the rancher as he was pulled away. The sudden fury left him like a sigh. He felt weak.

During the action Felipe Vasquez disappeared. Hawk Adams snatched Wingard's gun out of the holster before he got to his feet. Wingard got up shouting, and walked into his own gun as the marshal stepped before Jim and crowded the rancher into a corner.

"Whoa, now, horse!'' he said. He sounded amiable and absolutely confident. "You ain't going to bellow your way out of *this* one. It's got kind of serious, all of a sudden. Sit down. Don't stand there breathin' in m' face. I said sit down.''

Wingard turned a chair. ''What's the matter? Are you all crazy?''

''Where's Ed?'' asked Adams.

''At the ranch. I passed him going out as I came in this morning.''

''Where's his hat?''

''How would I know?''

''Did you bribe Vasquez to report it stolen?''

Wingard's glance thrust past the marshal to Jim's white face. After the sudden, scrambling fury Jim felt drained. Then the rancher glanced at Henry Coe.

''Judge, maybe you're still talking sense,'' he said. ''What's going on?''

''Jim's signed a warrant for your son's arrest,'' Coe told him. ''He lost his hat when he shot Mario Ámador. I daresay that's no surprise to you. The trick with Vasquez was hardly worthy of a smart man like you. But I suppose you were pressed.''

Slowly Wingard's hand went to a blue swelling which had formed under his eye. ''I don't know what you're talking about. Ed's been in town.''

''So Vasquez said. But when it came to swearing by his faith, he found he couldn't repeat the lie.''

Wingard stood up. ''Is that what started all the excitement—this man who's still wearing a prison haircut claiming he saw Ed kill Ámador?''

''That's about it,'' Adams drawled. ''That ain't saying it'll end in hanging, necessarily. They might decide he's crazy and send him to the lunatic asylum.''

''You're damn right it won't end in hanging! And it won't end in your throwing down on him when he comes in town.''

''Won't, eh?'' Adams smiled.

Wingard glanced at the case of curios against the wall, at the racked rifles and manacles hanging from a peg in the adobe wall. ''Ed will turn himself in,'' he said, ''but not in this town.''

"He'll be brought back to this town for trial," Judge Coe told him.

"Not while it's run by a marshal who hasn't gone to bed sober in years, and a judge who's prejudiced against my son. Make war on Ed, Adams, and you make war on every man of consequence in Frontera. You may jail him, but you won't be in office to see him tried."

He took his hat and walked out the door.

Adams began chuckling. "Just full of it, ain't he?"

"You could arrest him for those remarks," said Coe.

"That'd spoil everything," Adams said. "I want to see how far he'll go. I'm giving Ed until tomorrow morning to show up. Then I'm going after him."

"He might be heading for Mexico right now."

"Not Ed. He'll come back to get Canning first." He smiled at Jim. "Makes you feel kind of creepy, don't it?"

"Makes me wish I had a gun."

"It's not just Ed I'm worried about. His father is an even bigger danger," argued Coe. "Right now Jim is the greatest threat Wingard's ever faced. If Jim testifies against Ed, the boy will either hang or go to an asylum."

"Got Jim's affidavit, judge. You don't think I'd let little Ed off the hook, do you?"

"Not intentionally. But affidavits are subject to dry rot. By the time Wingard's lawyer got through with it, he'd have a jury doubting the sanity or honesty of the man who'd given it. Whereas if the witness is right there with his hand on a Bible—''

"I'd be real glad," Adams offered, "to lock the witness up for his own protection."

"Nobody," declared Jim, "will ever lock me up again—for my protection or anybody else's."

Chapter 19

AT FOUR O'CLOCK Jim said, "I'm sick of talking about it. I'm going to get some sleep."

He lay down on the floor of Judge Coe's office with a newspaper under his head. In a few minutes he fell asleep. He came awake with a start and scrambled to his knees. Someone had shouted his name. Crouching in the middle of the floor, he stared about the room.

"What's the matter, Jim?" asked the judge. He was still working at his desk, his chin resting in one hand.

Jim felt shaken and thick-headed. "I thought somebody called me."

"No. But you've been asleep two hours. Let's go get some dinner."

Jim sat down, rubbed his face with his hands, and the thickness came back to his head. "I'm not hungry. Maybe after a while."

Coe kept working.

"Your wife's going to be looking for you," said Jim. "What time do you usually quit?"

"I work all night when I feel like it."

"How's your wife feel about that? You don't usually take criminal cases, do you?"

"I take any case I feel right about."

Jim walked to the window. A warm evening breeze swept in, coming across the windmills and trees and rooftops of Frontera. A fine, restorative air to breathe.

"Have you got a gun here?" he asked. For it was

getting dark, and when it was dark a man could come looking for him.

"I've got a hog leg in my desk that would make a bulge in a large valise. Adams would spot it in one glance. And you'd be on your way back to Huntsville. On the other hand," conjectured the judge, "you wouldn't be carrying it if you left it on my desk and stayed here."

"I'm beginning to feel about this room," Jim said irritably, "like I felt about my cell. I made up my mind I was going to spend the rest of my life under a tree. Walls don't fit me any more. Ever have the feeling a room's getting smaller?"

"Not that I remember."

"I've heard men spend half the night trying to yell the walls back. The ceiling gets to sitting on your chest, they tell you. You can't breathe." He looked up. "You've got one of those descending ceilings right here, I think."

The judge looked at him queerly a moment, shrugged, and said, "Then we'll go for a walk."

If I'm going to be shot, Jim thought hazily, I don't want to be on my knees.

The judge began writing hastily on a scratch-pad. "I'll just send a note up to my wife."

Jim's mind finally came awake. He took the note from the judge. "I'm doing a lot of thinking about myself and not much about you," he said. "Go on home, Henry. Get your dinner. I'll be back in a couple of hours."

"Don't be so damned heroic. As long as you're with me, nobody's going to bother you."

"A crazy man might bother both of us. Ed's not far from crazy."

"No, but the two of us will give him twice as much trouble. You see, I can carry all the guns I want."

"Bet you can't hit anything with them," Jim chided him. "No, if he gets me, he'll have to do it before witnesses. I want it to be so open and shut the jury won't have to leave the courtroom. I'm going down to Pierce's and sit in a corner."

Coe squinted. "Is that a promise?"

Jim raised his hand.

Coe grunted and opened a drawer of his desk. "I don't really think Ed's going to get past Hawk, if he does come to town. But if he does—"

He was holding a very small pistol with a handle curved like a parrot's beak. "Do you know whose this was?" he asked.

Jim felt a sharp tug of emotion. "Be damned! It was my father's. I haven't seen it in years."

Coe handed it to him. "I suggested leaving it here for safe-keeping. If he really intended to give up gambling then he didn't need a pocket gun. And to be found carrying one wouldn't help his reputation as a cattleman. But there's a time and place for everything. This is the time for a house gun—and the place for it is your pocket. There's some shells around here."

Experimentally, Jim snapped the hammer a few times. The gun resembled a toy. Yet it was chambered for five forty-one caliber cartridges. After loading it he slipped it in the pocket of his denim jacket.

"I feel better already," he remarked. "A man likes to be dressed like everybody else, doesn't he?"

He walked onto the street. It was like standing in a cold and raking wind. Shackelford was locking up; the hard white glare of Pierce's gas-lights fell across the walk before the saloon; the alleys and vacant lots were shadowed; and horses standing at the racks had their ears up apprehensively. He knew it was the weather and the time of evening. But he changed his mind about going to Pierce's. He wanted to get off the main street.

Staying close to the wall, he walked toward the stage depot. When he saw Felipe Vasquez in the door of the cantina, he knew suddenly where he was going. Felipe was standing straight as a soldier, cleaning a lamp chimney with a piece of newspaper. He nearly dropped it when he saw Jim crossing the street.

"I didn't expect to see you," he told Jim.

"I didn't expect to be coming. I need something to eat."

"There's nothing much. Mexican dishes only—I guess my sister could—"

Jim pushed him inside. "Let's get off the walk."

"A friend of yours—a man you know," Felipe faltered. "Well, he's here too—Tom Elrod."

Jim stepped inside. Elrod sat in back at a table with an unlit candle. He was eating a greasy fold of tortilla dripping with chili. He stared somberly at Jim and wiped his right hand on his trousers. Jim took a table in the front corner, where he could watch both doors and Tom Elrod. Felipe stood at the bar.

"Bring me some tortillas," Jim said. "*Refritos*, if you've got them. And coffee. So this is where Ed's coming first," he said to Elrod, as the Mexican left.

Elrod kept chewing. A candle in a wall clamp illuminated his face. He looked drawn and tense. The small mouth was puckered under the long nose, the cleft in his chin was like a healed cut.

"Have a good ride in?" asked Jim pleasantly. He felt cheerful about the gun in his pocket.

"*Así, así,*" muttered Elrod.

"I suppose Ed thought he was shooting at me," Jim said.

"I wouldn't know," Elrod said. He rose, wiped both hands, and began fishing for money in the pocket of his tight levis.

"Finish your dinner," said Jim. "I won't spoil it. We don't have to talk."

Elrod tossed some coins on the table. He took his hat from the floor. At the door he paused to look at Jim.

"Get this clear: I just work on Walking W. They don't ask me about things. I only work there."

"You know what to say when they ask you about things in court. You sent me to Huntsville. You know how to dynamite a herd for the man that pays your salary."

Since it was foolish to lie to him, the foreman walked out.

"Felipillo!" Jim called. Felipe appeared in the curtained rear door to the living quarters. "Did you tell your sister what I want?"

"Yes, sir."

"Then stay out here where I can see you. I trust you about as far as I can kick a plaster cow." Jim scowled at the man as he moved with his slight limp down the back of the little green bar to his stool. Felipe dipped glasses in a bucket of water.

Jim ate hungrily, glancing up every moment at the entrance. In the rear, the curtain to the living quarters was drawn. He finished eating and moved to the table where Elrod had been. Some Mexicans entered, dusty from their work, talking rapidly in Spanish. When they saw Jim tilted back in his chair, watching them with pulled up lower lip, they left.

"I'm bad for business," Jim observed.

"*Sí*, señor," said Felipe woodenly.

"So that's some consolation, at least. What time is it?"

"Eight-thirty."

Eight-thirty. Good and dark now. Nothing to do but wait. Wait for Ed to come in, and Adams to drop on him like a bullet hawk. Or for Ed to come in and drop on Jim. Elrod had obviously been banking that Ed would come first to the Cantina Vasquez for a drink and a run-down on storm conditions by the local weather man, Felipillo. Since Mott Wingard had not shown up, it was likely he was waiting at Pierce's Big Corner Saloon.

Jim got to wondering about Elrod. He walked to the dusty front window and glanced at the stage depot, and there he saw him at the window of the waiting-room. Jim returned to the table. Probably Ed would stay out a little way until it got dark. Then he would ride in—maybe after fifteen or twenty minutes. At that rate he was overdue.

"Felipillo!" Jim said.

"*Mande?*"

"What kind of winter we gonna have?"

Felipe smiled and shook his head. He sipped some tequila. Then he seemed to tense. A man was walking down the side street.

Jim held his gaze. "Because if it's going to be cold," he continued, "I ought to be getting some warm clothes. What do you think? Will I need any more clothes than I've got? All things considered?"

Felipe grinned, his lips trembling. "I don't know. But I hear the squirrels are gathering nuts early this year. That's supposed to be a sign, I think. My father always watches the trees in the mountains. When there's more needles than usual on the firs, it means—well—I forget."

He was leaning against the bar as though to steady himself. Jim dropped his hand in his jacket pocket and cocked the little house pistol. Moving a trifle, he brought the gun out and laid it in his lap; his bandaged hand rested on the table. Felipe sagged back against the shelves, staring at him.

"Needles are a very important sign, too," Jim agreed. "When there's more needles on the trees in summer, it means there's going to be more needles on the ground in the fall. Given that information, what more could you possibly want?"

"I—I guess nothing." The Mexican straightened and tucked in his shirt tail. "Well, I guess I see what my sister is doing! A man's got to keep track of his women folk!" He gave a smothered snort of laughter.

"Then there's another *very* important sign," Jim continued gravely. "If the candles in a room flicker, it means a door has been opened. And if a saloon-keeper goes out back right then, the sign is pretty good that he's going to die. Did you notice the candles flicker?"

Felipe nodded.

Jim sat back. "Well, then, stay put. And keep on dipping glasses. And don't look at that back door or you may die."

In the rooms in back Jim heard a man's voice, and then

a woman whispering something excitedly. Then there was a stillness as fragile as glass.

"Go get Marshal Adams," said Jim gruffly. "Hurry up. If you cheat this time, I'll kill you."

Felipe swung his leg over the counter and hurried at a stiff, limping gait out the door. Jim heard him walking up the block toward the marshal's office. Again a man was moving behind the peeling, whitewashed partition. Jim saw the curtain stir; a hand moved it and a man stood in the opening, peering about the dim little cantina. Ed Wingard's thin-skinned features were red and shiny, and his beard was silky in the candlelight. His blond hair was tousled. Then he saw Jim watching him and with a quick smile he stepped into the room. His hand was on the butt of his Colt.

"Well, well, well, well, well!" he said gloatingly. He began to laugh. "You never looked for Santa Claus to come in the back door, did you?"

"Yes. I've been waiting since Christmas Eve," Jim told him. "What's on your mind?"

"Oh, a lot of things." Ed wiped his nose on his sleeve and continued grinning. "The badman from Huntsville: that's the big thing on my mind."

"What've you got against me, Ed?" asked Jim. "Do you really know?"

"Have you got a couple of hours?" retorted Wingard. "I could start telling you."

"Time's the only thing I have got, but you haven't got any time at all."

"Why not? I didn't kill that greaseball. Elrod did. And you ain't going to mess me up testifying that I did."

"Why don't you kill Judge Coe, too? Then there won't even be a trial. You've got this legal business nailed down tight, Ed. Kill all the witnesses and officials and we won't need any more lawyers."

Ed walked closer and Jim leaned back against the wall to give himself plenty of room. Frowning, Wingard tried to see Jim's right hand.

"Put your other hand on the table!" he ordered.

Slowly Jim shook his head. "Draw your gun, Ed. Drop it on the floor."

"When I draw it, I'll drop you on the floor. Get your hand where I can see it!"

Jim laid his hand on the table with the barrel of the little pocket pistol pointing at Ed's chest. Outside he could hear running footfalls, and a deep voice shouting.

"This way?" he asked.

Ed backed desperately toward the curtained doorway, but halted and went to one knee behind a table.

"Stand up!" Jim shouted.

Wingard's head and shoulders showed. His face was disfigured with chagrin. He was shouting something at Jim as he pulled his gun from the holster. The barrel struck the edge of the table and the gun went off into the floor. The candles went out with greasy puffs of smoke. The room was a black, resounding pit. Jim steadied the butt of the house pistol against the table and fired. In the flash he could see the man behind the table, almost obscured by powder smoke. He fired again and heard Ed Wingard gasp, and then a chair went over with a flimsy racket.

He slipped away and stood in the corner, blinded by the gun flashes. He stood there listening. In the rear, women were screaming. A horse plunged to a stop before the cantina. Ed was making no noise audible above these other sounds. Jim groped toward the door. He fell over a chair and went to his knees. He was so frightened and shaken he had a wild desire to run. He kicked his way through the smoky darkness of chairs and tables to the front, collided with the wall, and then saw the gray rectangle of the door. A man wearing spurs was striding toward it. Jim held the little revolver like a stone and waited with his arm raised. The running man slammed through the latticed doors and immediately jumped out of line with them. He lunged into Jim's arms, and Jim brought the gun down on his head. He grunted and went to his knees. Jim smelled the heavy rum-soaked cigar smell of Marshal Adams. He stepped over him and ran into the street.

After the dark cantina, the night seemed brilliant. A horse stood near the door, shying from Jim. A man was running down the road from Houston Street. Jim ran to the horse and swung into the saddle. He tried to wheel the horse, but it swung in the opposite direction. He gave it rein and spur and crowded it up the street which intersected Clay. At the next block he tried to rein it north toward Houston, and it swerved recklessly south. He made it turn a complete circle and came out of it heading north. At Houston he tried to rein it toward the hotel and it turned in the opposite direction. Then he understood: Adams had trained it to rein oppositely. He loped to the hotel. All along the street, from the hotel to the Big Corner Saloon, men were appearing, yelling questions. Jim looked up. There was a light in Coe's office.

"Judge!" he called.

At that moment Coe ran from his downstairs doorway. He saw Jim, and ran up to him. "Jim! Jim!" he cried. "What's happened?"

"Ed found me in Vasquez's place. I had to shoot him. God knows I took my chances."

"Of course you did!" Coe said. He sounded choked.

"Because what chance have I got now? I could let them kill me, or defend myself and go back to jail."

"I know," Coe repeated. "Listen! Take all that stuff of Mario's from Adams's office. Find Mario's father in Chihuahua City. Give him the things and tell him what happened. He'll help you until it's safe to come back."

"Okay," Jim said. Come back? He could never come back. For he had broken his parole—killed a man— committed all the wicked acts an ex-convict must never, never commit.

"I'll get word to you. Are you all right?"

"Yeah. Got a bigger gun than this on you, Henry?"

"Take one from the marshal's office as long as you've already taken his horse. God, Jim—" Coe's face broke into almost tearful mirth— ''if there was anything else you could have done—!''

''There was. I cold-cocked Adams!'' This crazy, jittery horse of the marshal's was backing and sidling, and it would begin pitching in a moment. ''Tell Ann for me, will you? How it was, I mean. He hunted me—I didn't hunt him.''

''*Adiós!*'' Coe said, as the horse reared and went half-pitching, half-running up the road.

Jim stopped at the jail. He ran inside. He could smell Adams here, his cigars, his bay rum, the rotten hole in his arm. He found Mario's belongings, but his revolver was missing from them. He tried the drawers of the desk but they were locked. Locked, also, was the rifle rack, and he attacked it with a chair but could not break it. He thought he heard a man running toward the jail, so catching up the canvas roll he ran from the office. The street was deserted. He remounted and started off at a lope. There were three cartridges left in the gun in his pocket.

Chapter 20

As Mott Wingard was leaving the cantina, Doctor Neeley drove up in his wagonette. Henry Coe was still in the saloon with the marshal, whose skull—unfortunately, in Wingard's estimate—had not been broken by Canning's blow. Coe had kept driving questions at Felipe Vasquez; Adams had taken several straight shots of liquor; and the roomful of men had pressed around Ed's body until Wingard had savagely struck at one of them. Then they had left him alone.

Alone. The biggest word in the world.

Alone was where you wanted to be until you got there. While Ed was still moving, he had tried to talk to him. At last he could not watch him any longer. He had closed his eyes and gripped his son's hand while he died.

Neeley asked soberly as Wingard stopped on the walk, "What's happened?"

"My son's dead," Wingard told him gruffly.

The doctor shifted his bag from one hand to the other. He looked embarrassed, pained, awe-struck. "I'm—I'm sorry. I'll have a look at him anyway. I have to fill out the death certificate."

Wingard slowly walked down the street toward Hammond's feed barn. Behind him, he heard an angry baritone voice bellowing. *"Who the hell took my horse?"*

Who the hell did he think took it? thought Wingard wearily. I wish I'd run him out months ago. For as much as anyone, Adams was responsible for Ed's death. Bedeviling him about drinking, about not being a model citizen. Reaching the feed barn, he found it in complete darkness. He stepped back from the double-doors and drew his Colt. After listening a moment, he stepped inside.

"Hammond!" he called.

Hammond did not answer. The horses were quiet and he did not think Canning could be hiding here. Canning would be heading off on a high lonesome, for the border. With the gun in his hand, Wingard moved along the line of box stalls, hearing the quiet movements of the horses. He reached his own horse in its stall and spoke to it; he had instructed Hammond not to remove the saddle. He did not see Ed's. He tightened the girths and led it out to the street.

Elrod had not appeared, and Wingard did not think he was likely to, for Elrod was supposed to have been on duty at Vasquez's. Wingard swung up, drew his rifle, and opened the breech. It was loaded. He had feared that Hammond might have gone patriotic and unloaded it. Wingard took a knife from his pocket and put a deep crosscut in the nose of each bullet. He had never used a dumdum bullet except with varmints which had been hitting his herds. But this varmint from Huntsville had hit his herd for the final time. This trash sprung from trash. This arrogant whelp of a tinhorn gambler. This bushmaster who had struck once and crippled his boy, struck again and killed him.

Rights and wrongs: he swept them from his mind like straw. The towering wrong of them all—the only factor that counted—was that a gambler had been permitted to live like a rancher until he thought he was one; and his whelp counted himself right there in the buckboard with God.

He heard Hawk Adams running down the walk toward the stable. Wingard jogged rapidly out of town. There was a high, frosty crescent moon. Whatever trail he took out of Frontera, Canning would wind up on the Cuero trail before morning. For that was the shortest way, by miles, to the river. Before long Wingard picked up Canning's trail where he struck the county road.

"Ah!" he thought, a deep peace settling through him.

He rode hard for a half hour until he reached some broken country forested with mesquite, where large rounded stones lifted through the earth. He halted the horse for a moment and listened. Then he heard the horse behind him. He rode deep into the brush and tied the pony, and ran back to lie on a rock with the road below him. He hadn't thought Adams would bring a posse along to bungle things for him, but it sounded as if there were several horses on the road.

Then he heard Hawk cry, "Hah!" and a squirt snapped. A horse went into a trot. The horse has smelled me, he thought; but old Dead-Eye hasn't. Well, he'll smell my powder smoke in a minute. How'd he ever get the name of Hawk? he thought with a small, dry grin. He laid his cheek almost affectionately against the gun stock.

While Marshal Adams was procuring a saddle horse, Judge Coe tapped five men in the crowd at Cantina Vasquez. "Come up to my office," he told them. In five minutes they were gathered there—Ira Moore, the banker; Ben Shackelford, the merchant; Pierce, the saloon-keeper; Horse Hammond and Doctor Neeley.

By that time Adams had acquired a horse, and as Coe peered down he saw him riding to the jail. "He's leading a pack animal," he told the others quickly.

They stood at the windows, smoking, chewing their lips, coughing. "What a night!" muttered Shackelford.

Coe turned. "Yes, and think of the night ahead of Jim!"

Shackelford frowned at the dark street where men came and went. "Well, he—he more or less made his own bed, you'll have to admit.

"Trouble just pulls some men like a magnet," he observed.

Hammond nodded. And Coe stared at them, growing

red. "You cowardly, miserable— *Get out of here!*" he barked.

Moore pulled himself up. "Is that what you asked us up here to tell us?"

"No! I had a simple-minded notion that I could swear you in as a sort of Vigilance Committee, in case Adams turns down our services. Now I see what a pack of cowards you are. Dismissed. Excused. Get out."

Spreading the skirts of his frock coat, Doctor Neeley anxiously sat down. "No, but what did you have in mind, Henry?"

With hopelessness, Coe regarded the mild, bespectacled soft-skinned face. For these men were completely house-broken. It was unlikely that pride and courage like Jim Canning's would ever put them under the gun, and how could you expect a sparrow to comprehend the problems of an eagle? He opened a closet door and found a rifle. He laid it on his desk and started searching for shells. While he opened and closed drawers, he talked.

"I've come to understand Jim Canning," he said. "I think he's behaved with the kind of courage men like us can only admire, without ever hoping to duplicate. Now he's had to kill a man to protect himself. He had no right to be carrying a gun. But like any man, he'd rather be a live law-breaker than a dead saint."

"Where'd he get the gun, I wonder?" Shackelford murmured.

"I gave it to him." Coe stared into the wonder—the pity, really—on their faces. "And I'm proud of it! A lawyer—and a judge—putting a gun into the hand of a criminal! But I'm also his friend. Until tonight, I'd have done the same thing for any of you. Until five minutes ago, I counted on your helping Jim out of this trap he's in. Because you all helped put him where he is tonight. Just a little support from you, and Mott Wingard would have put a ring in Ed's nose long ago. Just the slightest evidence that the metal in you wasn't all in your teeth, and Adams would have walked softer. You helped clip Jim's wings;

and then you told him to get out and fly.''

He found the shells and spilled them on the desk. Drawing the loading tube, he began to load the gun.

''So that was why I asked you to help him. Even though a domesticated breed of chickens like yourselves will never get into the kind of trouble Jim's in, I thought you might be glad to take a little risk to help him out of the bind you put him in.''

Shackelford rubbed his neck and frowned at his store across the street. ''I'm real sorry for Jim, Henry. Maybe we could help. Why don't we go down to Pierce's and talk it over? Nobody wants to go off half-cocked when he's takin' a chance like this.''

''You need time to find where you left your guts the last time you used them,'' Coe pointed out. ''But Jim Canning's got no time, and all the time in the world wouldn't help you fellows find your courage. If you've got any, it's always right on top where you can put your hands on it.

''Excuse me,'' he continued, carrying the gun to the door. ''I want to catch Adams. Maybe I can arrange a posse of barflies who don't know what they're getting into. Though for what he has in mind, I don't think he'd want witnesses. *Dead or alive* isn't in his book. *Dead—* that's the way he writes it.''

He hurried for the jail.

Two plaid canteens hanging from the saddlehorn, an extra bandoleer of cartridges, a couple of rawhide packs, a light blanket roll, a bottle of whisky he was just shoving into one of the packs: these and a look of quiet bliss were all the supplies Hawk Adams was taking with him. Coe accosted him before the jail. A few men were observing the marshal's preparations as he worked fast but coolly.

''You look well prepared,'' observed Coe. ''How long do you mean to chase him?''

''Never can tell, Your Honor,'' said Adams thoughtfully. ''He might decide to take a trip into Mexico.''

''Are you meaning to take his trail alone?'' demanded

Coe.

Adams glanced at him across the pack horse. "Don't I look big enough to handle him?"

"A posse is customary."

Adams coiled and folded the lead rope and prepared to mount. "A gang of amateurs would only spoil my caper. Sneeze when they ought to keep quiet. Get themselves killed and set their widows on me."

"What are you planning to do?"

Adams swung up. "Get Canning. What else?"

"Dead—or alive?" Coe held the bridle of his horse.

"That's right," smiled Adams. "Dead or alive! He killed a man tonight—broke his parole—stole my horse—slugged a peace officer. Sound like the work of a fun-loving child?"

"All you ever wanted was to kill him!" cried the judge. "And now you've been cheated of the chance to kill Ed Wingard. So how much chance does Jim have to come back alive?"

"It's all up to Canning," drawled the marshal, reaching down to disengage Coe's hand. "Dead or alive. Don't make a bit o' difference to me."

He rode past the men in the street and jogged his horse into the darkness.

Mott Wingard lay on the rock like a snake in the winter sun, patient and deadly. He breathed shallowly, covering with his rifle the bit of moonlit road visible through the mesquite. He could hear insects clicking in the brush, heard a mosquito singing about his head, but he did not move. Then he thought he heard brush crackling. Raising his head, he listened.

But now the horse had come into view, and he settled down and pressed his cheek against the walnut. Head high, the horse came along at an uneven, sidling trot. Wingard looked for Adams across his sights. He raised his head. *Damn him! Where was he?*

There! Wingard saw him—hunched over the saddle

horn with hardly more than his hat visible, probably having sensed what was wrong with his horse at the last instant. The hat was a good enough target. Wingard fired and the flash blinded him. The notched bullet whistled through the brush. He heard the horse begin to run. He rose swiftly and ran forward, levering another shell into the chamber.

"One chance is all you get, mister!"

Somewhere in the brush behind the rancher, Hawk Adams spoke tersely. Then Wingard knew he had fired at Adams's pack horse, with his hat balanced on the saddlebags. In blind shock, he dropped to one knee and looked for the marshal. Directly ahead of him, a red and yellow flower unfolded a ring of gauzy petals, its center a minute dark core. He was struck staggeringly in the chest and sat down, gasping. He raised his gun but it went off before he could aim. He saw Adams standing there, aiming at him. The brightness came again—again—again, as Adams pumped the shots into him. The last shot missed because he had fallen on his back. Adams stood over him, gazing down while he reloaded a rifle.

"You never did believe I meant it, did you, boy?" he said. "Next time you set out to kill a cat, make sure it's a house cat, not a wildcat."

Chapter 21

IN THE MOONLIGHT, Cuero Canyon was silent and frosty. For the last time, Jim passed the cliffs, caves, trees, and catfish holes which were part of his boyhood. For now he had done the thing which had put him beyond salvation. Yet he would not give himself up and trust to the justice of the courts or the mercy of a man-hunter with a bullet hole in his arm. He would hide—and run—and fight until he crossed the border. There he could put together some kind of life for himself. But it would not be among his own people, and he would never see Ann again.

He felt utterly alone, isolated from everyone else in the world. Other men were going through this final agony of trying to live by a senseless code; but they could not help each other. Each man had to fight it out alone. And however it ended for them, they lost, every mother's son of them.

An hour ago Jim had heard firing behind him. It had probably indicated the nervous brush-beating of a businessman's posse. Hard to say how many men Adams would bring along or whether he would travel alone. Or what Wingard would do. But it was easy enough to understand that Jim must travel as fast as possible. If they ever stopped him, he was finished. And Marshal Adams's appaloosa—this crazy cross-trained bronc with the disposition of a firecracker—was wearing itself out. Sweating and winded, it spooked at every quail that whirred up out of the brush.

He pushed down the canyon. He guessed that Adams would bring an extra horse. Adams had the disadvantage of being the attacker, the advantages of proper equipment and experience. Tonight Adams was doing the thing he did best. Jim was good on a cow hunt; Hawk Adams was good at hunting men. He tracked a man with the hot excitement of a hunter hearing his hounds tree a cougar.

The appaloosa began stumbling over the shallowest scoops in the trail. Jim woke it up with a slash of a branch he had cut. But in a few minutes it was faltering again, and each time he pulled its head up it would stop. Then he would have to spur it again. He fought it steadily but realized with a sick despair it would never carry him far enough or fast enough to take him out of Adams's reach. He felt a corroding hatred of the marshal.

For he had been forced by Adams into the shameful game Adams had to play now and then. It was his season for murdering; his night of the full moon, when every hawk and cat hunted until sunup; the bare-fist fight where the marshal wore brass knuckles and his opponent fought on his knees. Then Adams would ride back with another man's blood on him, file a notch on his Colt and ask, *"Now then, who's next?"*

He began to feel as strong an urge to beat Adams at the game as to escape him. To be the man who killed Hawk Adams, instead of another notch on Adams's gun. He had the eye, Adams would say, pulling down the corner of his eye with his thumb; the eye for killing with any weapon at any range, for tracking, for detecting guilt in a face. Did he ever get carried away by his hunger into pursuing a man too fast to be safe? Jim wondered.

As he rode, Jim considered the trail ahead, recalling where it was narrowest, brushiest, and most treacherous. But Hawk had cut his teeth on trails like that. No, he thought, I'll hit him just after he's passed such a stretch and thinks the going is clear.

He remembered such a place—just beyond the ledge where he had dropped on Mott Wingard.

He flogged the horse into a lope, but suddenly it stumbled. Jim went over the saddle horn and landed hard on his back. He heard the horse thrashing in the brush and scrambled away. When it had propped itself on its forelegs, he stepped in and seized the reins. One rein was broken off short. He whipped his belt from the loops and tied the loose end of the rein to the buckle. He mounted, but the horse limped badly on a foreleg. Jim suddenly relaxed. Now it was simple. It had all been decided for him and Adams. They were going to settle things in Adams's way, but in Jim's country.

Swinging back and forth, the creek seeped along a rocky bank for a few hundred feet and then recrossed to the other side of the canyon. At a narrow point where the rocks had resisted erosion, the creek ran full and deep. The trail took to the water. Jim reined the limping horse into the stream and kicked his feet clear of the stirrups. The creek bed was gravelly and with few rocks. The horse tried to drink. He quirted it on. They passed a dense thicket of willows on the left—the kind of cover which made a marshal's life perilous. On the right, a high, broken chimney of rocks leaned out over the canyon. A sensible man would get off here and walk forward a yard at a time.

Beyond the narrows, the appaloosa lunged up a slick ramp of stone which led from the water to the trail. Now the stream was at Jim's right. The iron clatter of the animal's shoes was muted by the thin soil of the trail. Jim turned his head to listen. He could hear nothing. He rode a short distance farther. By now there was no adequate shelter at either side of the trail. Thin ribs of stone trapped ripples of shadow on the ground and against the sheer hillside grew a few stunted cedars. You could not hide a blanket roll behind one of those rocks, he thought; and nothing but a bird could hide in the trees.

So it was a spot for a man-hunter to relax and push along to the next danger point.

When he reached another damp jungle of willows, he

tied the horse and borrowed the marshal's fine black-dot rope from the saddle. He probaby called it his hangin' rope, Jim reflected. He ran back to the spot he had chosen. Again he listened. Suddenly his heart began to thump. Horses were coming. More than one. Jim felt suddenly unsure of his plan. Maybe Wingard and a whole damned posse — with Hawk for the point of it! Well, he had bullets for two of them and a spare if he needed it.

He tied the rope to the base of one of the cedars. He backed across the trail and stretched the rope above it. Pulling it down through a split in a rock, he made a knot to keep it tight. Now he could hear the horses jogging along. He took the little revolver from his pocket and walked to a point about twenty feet up the trail. Behind a long, flat stone, he lay prone on the damp grass. The riders had halted above the willows. They were looking over the trail and trying to decide what to do. Although he expected to hear them talking it over there was no sound at all.

All at once he heard a pony squeal and dig out. Gravel peppered the willows like buckshot; the horse hit the stretch of water and its hoofs tore the surface. It came lunging on through the shallow water, passing so close to the willows that they rustled stiffly. Jim raised his head, realizing numbly that he had misfigured the marshal. Where he had thought he would go slowly, he was charging through like a regiment of horses. The pony burst through the fringe of willows and hit the hard stone ledge. Jim could see nothing of Adams but a small bulk above the horse's withers. The horse slipped and landed thunderously on its side.

He rose quickly with the revolver cocked. As the horse struggled up, he stepped forward, looking for Adams. He stopped. The animal carried pack saddles, not a rider. The rider was following on another horse a few yards behind, already slashing by the willows. Jim dropped flat. He lay absolutely still, his face against the wet sand.

The pack horse ran by him; then it must have seen the rope, for it shied and left the trail to crash through the brush and plunge into the stream. The saddle horse came up the rock shelf and halted. Water streamed from it. Jim heard it snorting. A man muttered something. Then the rider let the pony move forward, swearing in a relieved sigh and jogging down the trail. Jim felt the slight shock of the animal's hoofs as it passed the rock where he lay. He looked up and saw the marshal, erect and vigilant, his carbine raised. As he passed, Jim lifted the revolver. He aimed at the back of his head. But the trigger seemed to resist his finger. He squeezed harder.

He remembered that day in the store, Adams knocking him down and drawling with a wink at Tom Elrod, "It's people reaching for things and not getting them that keeps them poor." ...*Adams dropping a nasty little oakum string rotten with matter into a wash basin and telling him to empty it in the street....* *"Always reckoned there was something wrong upstairs with a knife fighter." The creed of Hawk Adams: "There oughta be just one penalty for assault with intent: life."*

Well, damn you—shoot! Jim told himself. Drop that great and courageous man from his saddle and tell them how you did it—from ten feet, with a house gun! But he could not make the hammer fall. And while he shook and sweated with buck fever, Adams rode out of range.

Suddenly he came to. Raising the revolver, he fired a shot in the air. Adams lurched up on the stirrups and the horse bunched its hind legs and jumped ahead. Its forelegs hit the rope and the animal wheeled wildly through the air, its hind leg kicking high. Adams landed on the trail in a flat, grinding slide. The horse came down on its back. Adams lay, moving painfully, and Jim sprinted after him.

Before he could reach him, the marshal sat up. He had lost his rifle and stared dazedly about him. Suddenly seeing Jim, he flopped on his side and drew his Colt. Jim left the ground in a dive. He hit Adams in the chest and the Colt roared. As they went down, Jim knocked the gun from the marshal's hand. In the action he lost the pocket gun. He sprawled beyond the marshal, rolled over, and came to his knees. Adams, too, was rising. On their knees, they faced each other at six feet. All at once both men saw the Colt lying on the ground between them. Jim heard Adams grunt as he dived for it.

The marshal's hands covered the gun and he began pulling it to him. Jim's hand closed on a stone, he smashed down at Adams's wrist and for an instant the fingers relaxed. Jim clubbed down again, but Adams yanked his hands away and the gun took the full impact of the stone. The Colt lay on the gound with the cylinder driven halfway out of the frame. Seeing it, the marshal groaned and started to scramble up.

Jim rose with him. For an instant both men were looking for the rifle. Jim saw it lying in a tangle of brush, but as he lurched after it the marshal stepped into his path and sank his fist into Jim's belly. Jim went back, gasping with pain. Adams rolled in with a long whistling left that missed Jim's head. Jim fell on him and hung on while Adams tried to throw him off. Strength came back, and Jim released him and chopped at the marshal's head. Adams took it on the ear and Jim stepped back. Now the marshal set his right fist and moved in, but Jim was ready for him and slowed him with a fist in the mouth, stopped him with another roundhouse on the side of the head. Giving ground, Adams began to loosen with a thawing of that iron determination. And Jim went to work with the heavy-shouldered stolidness of a wood-chopper, breaking Adams down to his knees, and throwing punches short and sharp to his head until he fell forward and lay still. He was not going to move for a while.

Jim secured the rifle. Adams's horse was on its side, helpless, and Jim shot it. Then he dragged the saddle away and looked for the pack horse. It had snarled its lead rope about a stump a few rods down the trail. Jim caught the horse and cut the packs from it. It was probably saddle-trained as well, he reasoned, and would carry him. He led it back.

He remembered Mott Wingard, and standing silently he

listened; but the canyon was still. He saddled quickly. As
he was finishing, Hawk Adams began to come to. He sat
with his back against a rock and watched Jim work. There
were red, skinned places on his nose and forehead and his
mouth was swollen. At last he spoke.

"You are the poorest damn shakes of a badman
Huntsville ever graduated. Why didn't you shoot me
instead of going to all that trouble?"

Jim was tightening the flank cinch. "Because I couldn't
shoot you in the back. Tried to, though."

"Back—front—side— What the hell— You don't
have to do it over your shoulder with a mirror, do you?"

"Well, I'm just an apprentice."

"Listen, boy, there ain't any apprentice gunslicks. If a
man can't do it right the first time, he ain't gonna get a
chance to study up. A badman's cooked hard—never
over easy."

"Not always. I was cooked easy."

"And now you're just cooked."

"Look who's talking," said Jim.

"And take a good look at a man who knows what he's
talkin' about. Anywhere you go, they'll catch up. If not
me, then somebody else."

"No they won't. Not in Mexico."

"The hell you say."

"Coe'll sell my ranch for me. I can live pretty good on
the other side."

Adams began to grin. "Maybe that bunch of psalm
singers will come to your rescue, Canning. Make me lay
off you for a while."

"Oh, they'll come, after they're sure it's safe and the
judge puts on the pressure. Not because they want to, but
because he'll shame them. But there's still Wingard.
Somebody should have shot Ed a long time ago, but that
won't take Wingard off my back while he buys up public
prosecutors and puts you on the stand. You see, even aside
from Ed, I can go back to jail for packing a gun. But I
expect you knew that."

"You sound like a feller that's started to savvy up," said the marshal approvingly.

"I think so."

What he had savvied up to at last was that in the big things you were always alone. People didn't mean to be cowards; they just couldn't take the big risks for anyone but themselves. But men like Coe and women like Ann—if you found them when you needed them—could keep your eyes from getting to look like Adams's.

When the marshal saw that Jim was through speaking, he growled, "Well, don't go to Mexico on my account. There was only one man I ever gave a damn for in that town, and he's dead now. So why the hell should I hang around? Old Coe'll be gunning for me anyway."

"Who was that? Who'd you ever give a damn for but Hawk?"

"Wingard," said Adams. "You always knew what he wanted. I got a kick out of watching him angle for it. Because sooner or later, I knew I was going to have him served up on a platter with an apple in his mouth."

"Wingard's dead?" asked Jim in surprise.

"He tried to jump me. He went for the pack horse trick you didn't. Look, why don't you keep that rent horse you're saddlin' and let me have my appaloosa? He'll carry me. I got plenty of time."

Jim glanced at him. "Fine," he said. "That's what I was going to do anyway. We're going to miss you around Frontera, though."

"Canning," Adams said bitterly, "you couldn't give me the town of Frontera if it was wrapped in red tissue paper. They can hang you or give you a medal. Don't make a bit o' difference to me."

Jim met the posse three miles up Cuero Creek. They had stopped to make coffee. He rode up to their fire before anyone noticed him. There were Doctor Neeley, Henry Coe, Ben Shackelford, Horse Hammond and some other men, and most of them were squatting close to the fire while they gazed in dull misery into the flames. An owl skimming the treetops made a harsh cry. The possemen started out of their dullness and looked up at the sky.

In all his life, Jim had never seen so many frightened men in one place. Probably every year for years they had been promising themselves to be courageous next year, to be outspoken and stand up for their rights, to hit a man who needed hitting and not smile at people they disliked. He wondered whether anyone in the world was pleased with the way he was. It seemed to him that for your first twenty years people were hammering you into one shape, and for the rest of your life you were trying to hammer yourself into another.

To be safe, he rode in with his free hand raised.

"Jim!" exclaimed Coe, scrambling up.

"Hello, judge," said Jim. "Howdy, boys."

"Where's Adams?" asked Coe. The other men were rising. They all looked embarrassed. On their coats they wore little badges.

"He's quit," said Jim. "If you want his affidavit, he's not far down the canyon. His horse went lame. That's how he caught up with me."

"He ain't dead?" asked one of the men.

"No, but I wish somebody'd ride down and get the story from him."

He looked at their faces. After all, he thought, I've got to live with them. He smiled into Coe's eyes and said, "He thinks he isn't appreciated any more. He's looking for a town that needs a tough marshal like him. There was only one man he really understood here, and he's dead now. That was Wingard."

"What happened to Wingard?" someone asked.

Jim dismounted and stood warming his hands. He knew their thinking was running along similar but separate lines. What did the rancher's death mean to each of them? What did it mean to the town Wingard had helped found, and then tried to rule?

Jim told them the story, as he had gotten it from Adams.

Then he said, "I could use some of that coffee."

Shackelford poured him a cup and thoughtfully added whisky. "What'll you do now, Jim?" asked the merchant.

"Ranch. After I collect those cows and deliver them."

"If there's anything you need," Shackelford mentioned, "just let me know. Take all the time you need to pay for it. There won't be any interest for the first six months, either."

"Thanks," Jim said. "I'll try not to overdo it. When you feel like riding, why not go on down to the ranch? There's plenty of food there."

All but the doctor accepted. "I'm afraid Ann may have driven out to my camp. She said she was going to. I ought to go back tonight—at least that far." He caught Jim's eye and said, "I wish you'd go with me, Jim. I want to look at that hand again, for one thing. And you know Ann would scalp me if I came back without you."

"Not afraid of your own daughter, are you?" asked Hammond.

"She's the one person I am afraid of," the doctor said.

He pulled the badge from his coat and slipped it in his pocket. The other badges began coming off quickly. It seemed as though no one wanted to be the last to be wearing one.

WANTED!
More exciting Westerns from
Frank Bonham